'Course three-one-five, sir,' reported the helmsman.

'Fifty feet, sir,' growled the Second Cox'n.

'Full ahead together.' The captain had one foot on the bottom of the ladder. 'Surface!'

Number One had a whistle between his teeth. When the needle in the depth-gauge passed the fifteen-foot mark, he blew it, and the hatches were flung open as the boat surfaced.

Blinding sunshine met them harshly after the soft artificial light in the submarine. There was the convoy, a straggle of nine or ten junks of varying sizes, just about right astern. Ahead of the convoy, broadside on to the submarine's stern, was one of the anti-submarine launches. She was much the same size and shape as the usual British type of motor launch, the bridge high for her length, quick-firing guns dotted about her bridge and stern.

Away from the island, between the convoy and the submarine and keeping abreast of the centre of the convoy, was a second craft of the same class.

It took an effort to absorb this picture, so suddenly in view and so different from the picture that had been forming in their minds while they were waiting under water, but habit and the clear-cut orders overrode the momentary strangeness.

The three-inch fired, and the enemy launch that had been ahead of the convoy swung away.

'They're running away, by God!' muttered the Captain.

'Right eight, up four hundred, shoot!'

D1431290

By the same author

ALEXANDER FULLERTON

Surface!

GRANADA
London Toronto Sydney New York

Published by Granada Publishing Limited in 1974
Reprinted 1974, 1983

ISBN 0 583 12295 7

First published in Great Britain by
Peter Davies Ltd 1953

Granada Publishing Limited
Frogmore, St Albans, Herts AL2 2NF
and
36 Golden Square, London W1R 4AH
515 Madison Avenue, New York, NY 10022, USA
117 York Street, Sydney, NSW 2000, Australia
60 International Blvd, Rexdale, Ontario, R9W 6J2, Canada
61 Beach Road, Auckland, New Zealand

Made and printed in Great Britain by
Collins, Glasgow
Set in Plantin

This book is sold subject to the condition that it
shall not, by way of trade or otherwise, be lent,
re-sold, hired out or otherwise circulated
without the publisher's prior consent in any
form of binding or cover other than that in
which it is published and without a similar
condition including this condition being imposed
on the subsequent purchaser.

Granada ®
Granada Publishing ®

To A.H.

AUTHOR'S NOTE

This story is the product of the author's imagination. Any similarity between characters mentioned in the story, and actual persons, whether living or dead, is purely coincidental.

Nor is there any connection between the ships and submarines which are mentioned in this story and any ships or submarines which actually existed. True, there was a flotilla of submarines with their Depot Ship at Trincomali, in Ceylon: but the Flotilla described here is entirely imaginary, and none of the officers or men of that flotilla are represented in any way in this book.

PREFACE

One summer evening, a few years ago, three or four of us were leaning on the rail outside the Wardroom of a submarine Depot Ship. We stood smoking cigarettes and looking down on our submarines which lay alongside. It was just after tea, and we were the Duty Officers of those submarines. You had been dead a year.

One said, 'It's time someone wrote a novel about life in submarines. There have always been lots of books about surface ships: people 'd be bound to be interested in these things.'

'Don't think it could be done. The story would be so enclosed, so limited.'

'Yes,' agreed another. 'And it'd be damned hard not to bring in all sorts of technicalities that'd be more than most people would trouble to read.'

I said that I thought it could be done, one way or another. I'd thought about it, for a year.

'Have a go, old boy. But if you get it published, I'll eat my hat and give you a fiver into the bargain.'

Well, I've tried, and this is it. I wish I could remember who it was that laid the bet: I'd like to see anyone trying to digest a well-used submariner's cap, and what's more I'd have that fiver. Nobody could say then that the book hadn't paid. Everything has to pay, in peace-time: that's one of the things you learn.

But that conversation was not the real reason for doing this thing. It was only the excuse for letting go on something that I'd wanted to do ever since I'd heard that you had been killed, so unnecessarily, in an accident, when the war was over. A stupid way for you to die. You would so much rather have had it in the way that you had so often seen it coming. But you were too good for them, then. They got you a mean way: alone, out of your element: none of us were there to share it with you.

So I wrote this. It's an odd sort of wreath for you, Sir: but you wouldn't have wanted flowers.

CHAPTER ONE

The submarine creeps quietly along, patrolling a mile or so off the coast of Sumatra, in the Straits of Malacca. This is the northern end, the widest part, the entrance to the Straits.

A fisherman on the shore stands for a moment staring out across the water that lies beyond the mud-banks. He is emaciated, this man, and clothed in rags, because most of the fish he catches are taken to feed the Japanese occupying troops. Lately they have increased their demands, since junk after junk, laden with rice and other food, has failed to arrive in the river-mouth. Some of the junks' crews, landing later in fishing-boats to which they have been transferred, have carried strange tales of Englishmen boarding them in the middle of the silent night, taking them into their ships which float under water and later putting them into any other smaller craft that they have encountered. They were given fine food in the Englishmen's ships, and some have said that they would be happy to repeat the experience.

The fisherman cannot understand these things. Turning slowly away towards the fringe of palm-trees, he remembers the pall of smoke that darkened the horizon a few days ago. The Japanese were always more angry when these things happened: no man could call anything his own, in Sumatra, when the Japanese were angry.

A haze of heat hangs over the mud-banks. There has been no breath of wind for many days.

Thirty feet under the surface of the Straits a young man lay dreaming on his bunk: he lay on his back, moving as little and as seldom as was possible, following the habit that he had learned in the interests of keeping cool. There was little comfort in a bunk soaking and reeking of sweat, even when it was your own. Yet this bunk was comfortable: he knew it well, saw it as a sort of haven in which he could think his own thoughts,

9

dream his own dreams. On patrol, the bunk was the nearest, the only approach to privacy. There were five bunks lining the sides of the submarine's tiny wardroom, and the space was such that any two officers could have stretched out their arms from their respective bunks and shaken hands across the wardroom table. When you were used to it, the lack of space was no disadvantage: you learnt to take up as little room as possible, you learnt to do what you needed to do with a minimum of inconvenience to your fellows.

You learnt to lie in your bunk and dream. Many people more or less live on dreams, and most people entertain them to a greater or lesser degree. At periscope depth the silence and the warm inaction of being off watch are conducive to deep and happy dreaming: being young, wanting something softer than steel, more understanding than regulations, you dream mostly about the next leave and about getting back to England, the girl on leave and the girl in England being of course distinctly different people. The one on leave is in Kandy, the ancient capital of Ceylon, where unless you've had the best part of a bottle during the evening you're liable to be woken and kept awake by the drums from the Temple of the Tooth. This girl in Kandy is surrounded by at least four hundred other officers who appreciate her as much as you do, and as a result the drums are rarely loud enough to wake you up, which is in its way a consolation. The girl in England is in many ways quite different, one of the ways being that she is fond of you, worries about you: she writes letters frequently, and she has none of the attraction of the girl on leave. She is, however, linked in your dreams with an old car, freedom of movement in a countryside dotted with your favourite pubs, the fact that you can rub your hand along the old wood of one of her father's five-barred gates and feel all England under your hand. That'll be when the war's over, and another dream is the actual going home and telling them you're on the way. This one takes you to sleep, where a real dream tells you there's a target, and when Jimmy wakes you by kicking you in the side as he slides down from his bunk, it's true, there's a target and the order's Diving Stations, stand by Gun Action for the nineteenth time.

A coaster steaming through the Straits with food for a Jap

garrison, shells for Jap guns, clothes and comforts for Jap soldiers, and it's going nowhere except to the bottom. From forty feet the submarine comes up like a cork, a rocket that hits the surface in an explosion of flying spray, wallows with the water streaming off her flanks. The hatches were open when they were level with the water, and the first thing the coaster knows of it is a shell that smacks in below the bridge: if they had a chance of living, that'd teach them to keep a better lookout. The shell kills the helmsman, smashes the steering-gear, and the coaster begins to swing off her course.

It makes a difference that she swings, because it throws the deflection out and the next round misses, while the coaster opens up with a light weapon mounted on the after end of her bridge. The water is perforated down the submarine's starboard side and something clangs off the aftercasing to scream away astern. Shift target to stop the danger, and when the fourth round goes home, the back of the coaster's bridge is shattered in an orange glow of flame. It was more than well placed, it was a lucky one and hit an ammunition locker. The submarine's gun is used like a surgeon's knife, shifts to a new point of aim, the water-line, to let some water in.

The coaster's bridge is well on fire, and the blaze spreads aft where one of the crew has just taken a spectacular and unskilful dive over the side. Later there may be time to pick him up, but now it's only business, Malacca Straits business. Shells are ripping in, and some of them are getting right inside the coaster's belly before they burst. You glance at the Captain, and he's grinning at you as though there was something funny about the way you look, your face black with the cordite smoke; and perhaps your face shows also that this is what you enjoy doing.

The coaster is settling lower in the water, and as you blow your whistle in short blasts that tell the Gun's Crew to cease fire, her bow sweeps up and her stern goes down, down, the sea hissing as it drowns the flames and swallows the ship. Eleven minutes from the time the Gunlayer first pressed his trigger the submarine is alone on the surface, with a haze of smoke and some rubbish floating where the ripples spread, spreading till they lap the steaming mud-banks where the fishermen's stakes stand stiff like sentries that have witnessed an execution.

11

The Gun's Crew are busy clearing the platform of empty shell-cases, kicking the hot cylinders over the side, then training the gun fore-and-aft and jamming on the clamp. Shells come up from below to refill the water-tight ready-use lockers, the Gunlayer and Trainer unship their telescopes, and the five men drop down through the hatch, which clangs shut as the submarine heads back to pick up the one Jap survivor. He's clinging to a plank which he must have thrown over before he dived. Two sailors drag him up over the saddle-tanks, and he's so dazed that he tries to bring his piece of timber aboard with him. He's a lucky man, because everyone knows that the Japs have no healthy interest in our survivors, and he might not be welcomed as a guest were it not that the Intelligence people will like to have a chat with him. Moreover, he ought to be ashamed of himself, because in between being sick he mentions that he was the Captain of the ship. The best captains stay in their ships at least as long as the rest of their men.

The submarine turns and heads out towards the middle of the Straits, twelve knots and the bow-wave curling away as white as spilled milk. White shows clear and far on the dark blue surface, and the sinking will by now have been telegraphed to a Jap airfield, so while the submarine must put herself out in the deep water as quickly as her diesels will get her there, she must also have an eye on the sky. Within a matter of twenty minutes this sky holds three little specks growing bigger from the direction of Penang, but they have little time to get much bigger before the bridge is cleared, the vents drop open in the saddle-tanks and the submarine glides down until the needle in the depth-gauge is steadied at fifty feet. An order from the Captain puts the wheel over to starboard, swings her round towards the South, towards the One Fathom Bank and the minefields that guard the road to Singapore.

Look at a map of the Straits of Malacca and you'll see, if the map is large enough, that where the Straits narrow about half-way down to Singapore is a lighthouse marking the One Fathom Bank. South from this point the way is barred by belts of submarine mines strung across the channel between the sand-banks. There are many belts of them swinging to and fro on their wire moorings, live things waiting in the dim, green silence, death in their horns and antennae. For nearly three years no submarine has passed south of the One Fathom Bank. One day, someone will have to be the first.

Back to zero again, with the figure twenty in the front of your mind, or at the back of it. Twenty is the number of rounds it took to sink the coaster and to kill four Japs who would rather have died than lived, which they could have done by jumping with their captain when they knew their ship was one for Davy Jones. Thinking around their preference for dying it was almost understandable that they often killed prisoners instead of marching them into cages, because they seemed to have the impression that a prisoner was a deader man on his feet than he was when stiff. It did not cover their habit of twisting bayonets round in a man's stomach when he lay with rope round his ankles, though, and it was knowing of such habits as these that made it easy to kill Japs without considering them as being any more than monkeys with a blood-lust.

Twenty was something else as well, more personal, the age of the girl in England. Strange, that while you're lying on a narrow bunk fifty feet under the surface of the Malacca Straits the girl may be playing a game of tennis in Sussex on a grass court that you helped to weed. To be honest, why think about her at all, when you know that it is only needing someone to think about that makes you do it about her? In your mind you are remembering not the look of her, but the look of Crowhurst, Heathfield, Manfield and Cross-in-Hand, smelling the sweet tang of an early morning in the woods behind Buckholt. It was having someone, too, that you could know was thinking about you, a contact in the outside world where people used thin china and kept themselves clean and didn't have destruction as their aim from day to day. When you heard Stuart Someone-or-Other reading the B.B.C. news and saying that a certain tonnage had been sunk by His Majesty's Submarines in the Far East, you immediately thought of her listening and knowing that this was what you had done, and you were in her mind and she'd care if your letters stopped reaching her. That was why you thought of her, and you knew that when you were home

13

and the war was over you'd see no more of her than of anyone else.

'What colour are her eyes, Sub?'

What colour? Grey, or green, or the mixture called hazel?'

'Whose eyes?'

'Don't tell me you weren't mooning over Sheila.'

Sheila: she was the girl in Kandy, and you knew about her eyes. Green they were, like a cat's eyes in the dark. After this patrol you were due for leave, and you hoped to be seeing something of those eyes. When you got back: it never occurred to anyone that they might not get back from this patrol, or the next, or the one after that, and if it did occur to them they thought about something else, because imagination is an enemy under water and there are enough enemies without making your own.

'What's for supper, Chef?'

The cook shoves his head round the side of the water-tight door, an opener in his left hand menacing the tin in his right.

'Bangers, sir.'

'And mash, I hope.'

'Yes, sir.'

The Captain looks up from the signal-pad over which he has for some minutes been aimlessly waving a pencil.

'Bangers? You mean Soya Links, don't you?'

'That's right, sir.'

'Christ! Again?'

Chef looks at Chief, the Engineer Officer, an expression of pain and surprise on his unshaven face.

'Don't like links, sir?'

'I'll have yours, Chief.' Chef transfers his gaze to the Sub-Lieutenant. His expression says, 'Ah, you're all right: proper sailor's taste.' He looks at the Captain. 'What time we going up, sir?'

'About an hour. Tell the Cox'n I want him.'

'Aye aye, sir.' The Captain doodles on his signal-pad until the Cox'n heaves himself through the bulkhead door.

'Yes, sir?'

'We'll surface at eighty-thirty, Cox'n.'

'Aye aye, sir.' He pauses. Then,

14

'Nasty little bastard we got for'ard, sir.'

'Which?'

'The ruddy Jap, sir. Sullen cove. They got 'im peelin' spuds, but I don't know as it's right lettin' 'im 'ave a knife.'

'Make him use a short, blunt one. And have the fore-end watch-keeper keep an eye on him.'

'Aye aye, sir. Shadwell's looking after him now.' Everyone smiles. Shadwell could look after an army of Japs and they still wouldn't try anything.

The Cox'n turns and walks for'ard. You slide off your bunk, tighten the belt of your shorts and go barefoot into the Control room to take over the watch. The Captain's buzzer buzzes and you nip back to the Wardroom.

'Red lighting at eight, Sub.'

'Aye aye, sir.' No dreams now, only trim, course, speed, position and a careful periscope search as the light fades over the Straits. Keep an eye on the man with the headphones: what eyes can't see, ears can hear. They are big, hairy ears, and even the frequent wearing of headphones for hours on end has failed to prevent them standing out at right-angles to the man's head. He's a nice lad, Saunders, a farmer from Dorset, and he'll be glad to get home one day to a decent pint of bitter, if it'll ever be decent again, and not just coloured water. That's what the Germans have done, thought Saunders, watered the bloody beer, them and the Nips between them. Tortured old men and women too, killed little kids, and you couldn't sit by and let 'em do that, not without having a bash at them, the dirty bastards.

Eight o'clock on the Admiralty-pattern electric clock. White lights are out in the Control Room and in the Wardroom, red ones glowing in their place. Red light, say the scientists, accustoms the eyes to seeing in the dark; so do raw carrots, which are eaten whenever anyone remembers to eat them. The Captain wears dark goggles as he pulls on a waterproof jacket, then gropes behind the water-tight door for his binoculars. The First Lieutenant takes over the watch, and the Sub, who will have the first watch when they surface, gets dressed and studies the chart in the dim orange light.

Eight-fifteen. Number One, in the Control Room, reaches for the microphone that hangs from an air-pipe on the deckhead.

15

He flicks the switch on with his thumb and says:

'Diving Stations.... Diving Stations.' Within a minute each man is in his place, his station for diving, surfacing, attack. Again the microphone carries an order through all compartments:

'Stand by to surface.' Reports come in, vents shut, blows open.

'Ready to surface, sir.' The Captain is straining his eyes into the periscope. The man with the headphones, Saunders, reports all clear all round. The periscope hisses down into its well, and the Captain puts a foot on the ladder as the Signalman steps back from opening the lower hatch.

'Surface!' High-pressure air rips into the ballast tanks as the hydroplanes are swung to force the boat up. The needle in the depth-gauge rises, slowly at first, then faster, and the Captain and the Signalman climb up through the hatch into the conning-tower. As the submarine breaks surface the Captain opens the top hatch and heaves himself quickly up on to the bridge. The diesels roar into life and the submarine gathers way through the dark deserted sea: her sleek hull gleams shiny black while the water still drips from her sides. Down below in the warm, lighted compartments men are lighting the first cigarettes and pipes of the day. The comfort and sociability of smoking draw men together, and in this strange world of their own, remote from others of their kind and near only to their enemies, men from all walks of life and all parts of Britain are perfectly at home.

Stand alone on the front of the bridge while the submarine forges slowly ahead, one engine driving her at slow speed while the other pumps new life into the batteries. There are two seamen, lookouts, on the after end of the bridge, binoculars at their eyes, but you, the Officer of the Watch, must see anything before they see it. The Captain is asleep, or as near asleep as he ever is, down below, and in these narrow Straits which are enemy territory you alone are responsible for the safety of the ship and the lives of the men in her. For the two hours of your watch the binoculars are never lowered from your eyes, not for

16

longer than it takes to pass an order or quietly to acknowledge a report through the voice-pipe: to and fro and all round the glasses sweep, minutely careful, missing nothing. You must see the enemy, if he is there, before he sees you, and if you fail in this you can call yourself a failure and there is no place for you in a submarine.

As you sweep, questions ask themselves and are answered automatically in your mind: What will I do if I see a dark shape there, a bow-wave there, coming towards at speed? If a strange recognition signal challenges from the darkness on the starboard bow, what action will I take? What will be my first order down the voice-pipe if I hear an aircraft which the Radar has failed to pick up? Watchful, straining eyes, a tense mind and a body taut and hard, only the regular swish of water sweeping over the saddle-tanks and the low throb of one diesel breaking the silence of pitch-black night. Over all, the constant hope: an enemy worth sinking, and you must sight him not one second later than it is physically possible to sight him. That is all you have to do, alone on the bridge, and to every detail you must do it, because you are part of something in which only the highest standards are acceptable.

This is Patrol Routine.

Remember how it started? In a garage, for you, on the same Sunday, of course, when it started for the rest of the world. You were making screens for blacking-out the windows, tacking thick cardboard on to frames of thin deal slats that you'd make to fit the windows. You were the son and the only male of one of thousands of households that were getting ready for a war. You knelt on the garage floor, that summer morning, and hammered in the nails while your mind was full of the war which, being very young, you had been looking forward to for some time.

You were on leave from the Royal Naval College at Dartmouth. In a year or so you'd be at sea as a midshipman, and you hoped the war would last that long so you could go to sea and fight and make up for having thoroughly disliked the time you spent at Dartmouth. Not that it was your fault, really. At the age of thirteen the brass buttons and a photograph in the *Illustrated London News* had been enough to give you night-mares of failing the entrance examination. Besides, there was an Admiral with your name, and there had always been your name in the Navy List, so they said, your aunts and your mother, that is. So when you were thirteen you went to Dartmouth, in a uniform, and you were told that you were a Naval Officer and that you were expected to behave as such, but when you arrived at Paddington on your way home after the first term and you strolled into the refreshment bar and asked for a sausage-roll and a pint of bitter the barmaid smiled and said, 'Sorry, sonny, no beer, not under eighteen.' You were still a little boy, after all. Your House Officers didn't think so, though, or else he had less idea than his job demanded of how to treat little boys. He sent for you one day, during Stand Easy, and you ran up the narrow stairs wondering what it was that you had done now.

'Shut the door,' he said, and you shut it, taking care not to let it slam, and you faced him squarely, ready for something.

'When did you last see your father?' he asked, abruptly, as though the question embarrassed him. It struck you as being a silly question, and you had a quick flashback to the picture of a little boy standing on a hassock in front of the Roundhead officer who was doing his job of hunting down Englishmen who had committed the crime of loyalty to their Sovereign. You gave him the obvious, the only answer.

'Last leave, sir.'

Your House Officer put his hand flat on the desk and stared at the back of it. Then he looked at you, and you felt as though he didn't believe you. He said:

'Well, he's dead.'

There was a pause, while you looked into his impersonal eyes: you felt no emotion because it had come so quickly. He looked away, back at his hand, and he asked, still looking at it:

'I suppose you can carry on with your work?'

'Yes, sir,' your voice said, and your hand turned the knob on the door and your feet took you down the stairs, running, be-cause otherwise you'd be late for the class, and there would be no excuse for that when you had said that you were able to carry on with your work.

Lots of other boys loved Dartmouth, and that made you feel very different, abnormal. If so many were happy, it must be you that were wrong. So you always said, when they asked you how you liked it, that you loved it, every minute of it, and they always believed you.

And you felt you ought to like it.

The big screen for the french window in the dining-room was just finished when your sister shouted from the drive that the broadcast was coming through, and you dropped the hammer and ran with her into the drawing-room, where your mother was sitting as stiffly as though she were sixty and not thirty-five. The Prime Minister spoke, said that a state of war existed between us and the Germans, and then they played the National Anthem and you stood to attention, which you had been taught people never did in their own homes. Your mother looked as if she was going to cry, so you left as quickly as you could to finish the job in the garage. You knew that what made her unhappy was the fact that you would soon go to sea and stand a chance of being killed, and this was something you couldn't deal with because what made her so miserable was the very thing that made you happier than you could remember.

A few years ago, whatever you felt, you could have cheered her up, shown her that you loved her and made her believe that things would be all right. But now: well, you'd been to Dartmouth.

A thin trail of exhaust from the throbbing diesel curls over the submarine's wake. The tense, watchful atmosphere of the night patrol hushed your voice so that you speak quietly into the voice-pipe, although if you shouted no enemy could possibly hear. A lookout pauses to wipe the sea dew from his binoculars with a wad of periscope paper. It is half-past one, and in half an hour the watch will be changed and you can go below to sleep until, just before the light comes, the submarine dives for the daylight patrol. For the three weeks of the patrol you follow the same routine of two hours on watch, four hours off, except for the times when your off-watch spell is broken by the alarm buzzer, or the klaxon, or the sudden shout of 'Diving Stations' that means an attack. When it means an attack, you're glad to be woken, however tired you are.

Sweep all round for the thousandth time, blink and start again at thirty degrees on the port bow, sweep slowly right, over the bow and down the starboard side, stop at about thirty degrees on the bow, sweep left again. Stop with a jerk at ten on the port bow: something darker than the night. No good staring straight at it or you'll lose it, sweep to and fro just across it, don't act until you know it's real and not one of those things that are so easy to see in your imagination when you're looking for them. This one is real. Note the bearing, keep your glasses on it while you order one of the two lookouts to get down below. Into the voice-pipe:

'Stop starboard, out engine-clutch, break the charge. Captain on the bridge. Stand by all tubes. Night Alarm.'

Down below your orders are shouted through the compartments and you hear the buzzer making long buzzes, an urgent, penetrating noise like a dentist's drill in a sleeping sailor's brain. The Captain's on the bridge and you show him the target, but it's a full minute before he gets it in his glasses.

It could be anything from a junk to a destroyer. Send down the other lookout: you may have to dive in a hurry. It's not likely to be a destroyer, but from this angle it looks damn like it. Slow ahead on the motors, creep round the target at the same distance. Whatever it is, it's under way, started on the port bow and has crossed to starboard, moving very slowly, but that's no indication as to what it is because even a destroyer can go slowly when it wants to, when, for instance, it's hoping that a submarine may be in the neighbourhood on the surface. Creep round, watch the target. Close in from astern, and suddenly, as clearly as though it was daylight, you can see that the tallness is not the superstructure of a destroyer but the sails of a big junk.

Voice-pipe again:

'Stand by Boarding Party.'

'Carry on below, sir?'

'Yes.' You fall through the hatch on to the ladder and drop into the Control Room, move aft quickly through the hurrying

20

men. Over your bunk in the wardroom hangs the belt with a ·38 revolver and a short Italian bayonet strung on it. Grab the belt and strap it on as you check up on the Boarding Party who are mustering in the Control Room. They're all there with their gear: revolvers, heaving-lines, a wheel-spanner, and Shadwell the Torpedo-man has a bag containing two fitted charges, lighters and a pair of pliers. That's all you need.

'Boarding Party ready in the Control Room, sir.'

'Very good. Come up, Sub.'

On the bridge again, you see the junk plainly, even without binoculars. She's right ahead with her stern towards you.

'Up Vickers guns.' Two seamen appear out of the hatch and mount machine-guns on each side, slap on the pans of ammunition and stand ready.

'Boarding Party on the bridge.' They pour up through the hatch, five of them.

'Ready, sir.'

'All right, Sub. Down you go.' The Captain hasn't taken his eyes off the target for one second since he first saw it. He stands hunched in the front of the bridge, a silent, familiar silhouette of a man as you swing a leg over the side of the bridge and climb down the cut-away footholds on to the catwalk, walk around the side of the bridge on to the fore casing. The men are behind you and you lead them for'ard, right up on to the sharp bow, between the anchors. Crouch down so that the Captain can see over your heads, and watch as the distance lessens between you and the stern of the junk. The submarine is propelled by her electric motors, and there is no sound except for the swish of the sea under the bows and over the tanks, and as you get closer you hear also the creak of the junk's gear. The submarine's bow swings off a foot or two to starboard and suddenly with the slightest of bumps you're there, the high wooden poop towering over you, and you jump, your hands grabbing the top edge of the junk's stern rail. Swing over, land quietly on the poop, your rubber-soled shoes make no sound. The men are behind you, swarming over.

'Sails down, Bird.' The Second Cox'n and two others run to the mainmast, hack at the ancient cordage, and as you throw open the door of the shelter in the poop, the yard crashes down across the junk. A light line holds the submarine's bow along-side.

There are three Chinese in the shelter, screaming and shouting, scrambling over each other, mad with fear and excitement.

'Shut up! Speak English?'

'Yes, master.'

'Good.' One of the Boarding Party is behind you. 'Get these Chinks aboard.'

'Aye aye, sir.' The crew are hustled away. The junk's papers are in an old box in the corner, and you stuff them into your pockets. Out of the shelter, you drop down into the after hold, Shadwell with you. Using the bayonet you prise up a board, and under it six inches of dirty water cover the bottom of the ship.

'Five-minute fuse.' Shadwell chops off the right length of fuse and you drop the charge into the water. The old junk creaks and groans as you work by torchlight, preparing to send her to the bottom. All set, you scramble up on deck, and shout,

'Ready, sir!'

'Carry on!' the Captain's voice hails back out of the darkness.

'Clear the junk.' The Boarding Party jump down on to the submarine's casing: you retire alone into the hold with Shadwell's pliers to fire the tube on the fuse and finish the job. Shining your torch down through the bottom boards you kneel there to check that the charge is in the best spot. There's a grunt in the dark over your head and you spring back, your torch lighting up a Jap face with a snarl on it, a yellow hand with a knife in it. The Jap has been hiding on top of the cargo, dragging himself laboriously forward through the narrow space between the top of the stack of cases and the deckhead. Another foot, and he'd have had you with that knife. The ·38 jerks in your hand as you fire twice, and one bullet gets him just above the left eye. He slumps forward, dropping the knife, which is big and heavy: it falls on the boards where you were kneeling a moment ago. You hardly notice that blood is dripping from him as you dive down to the boards again, grab the pliers and fire the fuse: see it begin to splutter then get away fast, jump down on to the submarine's bow and flash your torch at the bridge. The submarine backs away from the deserted junk that hasn't long to live.

A minute passes and the Captain mutters, 'Should have gone off by now.' You've been thinking the same thing. Another minute passes and there's a *whumph* and the junk's stern lifts a clear foot in the water, then drops back and she begins to settle. Just after two o'clock there is no junk left, and the Captain asks whose watch it is.

'Number One's, sir.'

'All right, Sub. Tell him to come up when he's squared things off.'

'Aye aye, sir.' You would also like to square something off, with a Chinaman who talks English but can't tell you when there's a guard on board. You ask him. He says that he was frightened and forgot, and that when the Jap wasn't taken away with them he thought that he'd been disposed of and he hadn't liked to ask questions. The Chink looks hurt when you tell him that he's a bloody fool.

You drink a cup of the Cox'n's cocoa before turning in, and while you drink it you look through the junk's papers, spread out on the wardroom table. Her cargo was rice and small-arms ammunition, and had been meant for Burma. By the light of the single red bulb in the wardroom you parcel the papers together in a big envelope and stow them away in the correspondence locker. The Captain will need them to put in with the Patrol Report. You open your drawer and take out the Torpedo Log and Progress Book, on a spare page at the back of which is a record of torpedo stores expended: you write in neatly the date, 'one 1¼ lb charge, fitted', and in the last column, 'one junk, about eighty tons'. Blot it and close the book, and you realize that you're still wearing your belt: you slip it off, take the four unused cartridges out of the revolver and stick your head round the bulkhead into the Control Room. The Gunlayer is on watch, sitting on one of the planesmen's seats, waiting to go up and relieve a lookout.

'Clean this for me, will you, Smith.'

'Aye aye, sir.' He flicks it open and squints through the barrel at a light.

'Used this tonight, sir?'

'Yes.'

'Kill the flipper, sir?'

'Yes, just before he killed me.'

'Blimey. Would they've made me Gunnery Officer, sir, if you'd copped it?'

'Flippin' likely,' mutters the Cox'n. 'Ninety days is all I'd give you, you bastard.'

'Speakin' of parentage,' replies the Layer, gazing into the barrel of the revolver again, 'I 'ave always made an 'abit of being very polite to Cox'ns, but recently I 'ave to admit it's been flippin' 'ard to keep it up.'

'What I've been wondering,' muses the Cox'n, jerking his thumb up towards the deckhead, 'is what the 'ell we carry a gun up there for when there ain't nobody in the ship's company with the slightest flippin' idea of 'ow to work it.'

'If I was the Gunnery Officer,' answers Smith, 'I'd take exception to that remark.' But the Gunnery Officer has gone, and is climbing into his bunk when the Captain stumps in, discarding a wind-jacket.

'Did I hear some shots, Sub, when you were down below?' You turn and look at him.

'Yes, sir. Two. A Jap was creeping up on me while I was fixing the charge.'

'You fired both the shots?'

'Yes, sir. He had a butcher's knife.'

'You'd better type a statement, and I'll put it in with the report.'

'Aye aye, sir. Diving at five?'

'About then.'

That had been another good twenty-four hours for the *Seahound*. She was a lucky ship: some submarines had the damnedest luck, patrol after patrol without a glimpse of the enemy. *Seahound* had never yet had a blank patrol: each time, when she returned to her base, she had been able to fly the Jolly Roger, and always the flag bore some symbol of a new success: a bar for a ship torpedoed, a star for one sunk by gunfire. Even the very first time, the 'working-up' patrol in the North Sea, when *Seahound* had been sent to patrol a quiet area where there was little likelihood of any excitement. The object was to give

24

her men a chance to settle down to each other and to their new ship, to get used to the routine of patrol. They weren't expected to sink anything. But from that patrol they returned in triumph with a red bar sewn on the virgin Jolly Roger, red for a warship, a big U-boat which they blew in half with a torpedo, on a dismal rainy morning with the visibility so low that from the time of sighting the U-boat to the time of firing the salvo the hands of the Control Room clock covered only six minutes. The U-boat sank in two separate parts, and *Seahound*'s Captain jumped up and down like a little boy at the periscope, shouting, 'We've got her, by Christ, we've got her!'

There was a warm welcome from the Depot Ship when a week later they slid into the Loch, and there had been frank surprise in many faces. The Seahounds were due for leave, a last leave in England before they sailed for the Far East: the officers were all going south, to London, and they left together in the Depot Ship's motor-boat, passed close to their submarine which lay alongside and on whose casing Number One stood to wave farewell: he had had his leave, before the last patrol, and now he regretted having taken it. The boat jumped and bounced through the choppy grey waters to the landing-place near the Bay Hotel, and the Seahounds had time for a drink in the American bar before they caught their train for Glasgow.

Of course, none of them got sleepers at Glasgow. It was the usual routine: the man in the office said they were all reserved, for Generals and Very Important Persons, but that when the train started the attendant might be able to help them. In other words, any sleepers that remained would go to the highest bidders.

The Captain said, 'Not worth enriching the attendant. May get a compartment to ourselves, if we're quick.' They found an empty First at the front of the train, and while the Captain and Sub were stowing their cases in the racks, Chief opened his and drew out a small T-shaped metal object. He inserted it in the keyhole of the door and turned it.

'I've had this since I was a midshipman,' he told them. 'Pinched it from a guard. I used to have some stickers with "Reserved" printed on them, but I've used them up.' The train lurched and gathered way, southward bound: they had a corner each, plenty to read, a set of dice and a bottle of whisky.

The train stopped at York. Just before it was due to leave, the Captain ordered Sub to go and buy some sandwiches. There was a fighting crowd round the refreshment barrow, and he had just got his food and his change when the train shrieked and began to move. He ran, clutching the paper bag, wrenched at the door of the last carriage, but it was locked or jammed. He threw the parcel into the dark window and followed it, head first, landing heavily on a sailor and a girl. It was Able Seaman Young, of the *Seahound*. Young cursed, and the girl screamed.

'Sorry, Young. Nearly missed it.'

'Nothing doing, Mr Ferris. You'll 'ave to find one of your own: this one's mine.' The truth of his statement was only too obvious.

They seemed surprised when he eventually turned up.

'Thought we'd have to go hungry. What d'you get?'

'Sausage-rolls. You ought to see Young's girl-friend. I'd like to be Young, till London.'

'Trust a torpedoman,' observed the Captain. The train rattled and rumbled into the south. Throughout the length of it soldiers, sailors and airmen dozed and slept. Most of them were going on leave: some for a week-end, some, just home from overseas, for a longer, gay, embarrassing reunion: some, like the Seahounds, to say good-bye to people and things that they had always known and might not know again. The train was part of the war-time life: whether the end was an end or a beginning it was all the same to the engine: crash, rattle, wallop down the line, down to London and the fleshpots of the south.

Early morning in London: the train stood steaming, exhausted, in a grey station that smelled of hangover. Long after the other passengers had dispersed, Very Important Persons slumbered on in their sleepers. They were getting the Government's money's-worth. The attendants brewed tea, and waited for tips.

The Sub leant forward to hear what the taxi-man was saying. He was a stranger in Ambershott, and any local information would be of interest.

'You'll find it a bit of a dead-end up there, sir.'

'Dead-end?'

'Ah, sir. Quiet. Big old 'ouses, they are, quiet as the grave, you might say. Which p'ticular 'ouse, sir?'

'It's called Tregowan.'

'Tregowan, sir?' The old head whisked round in surprise, and the taxi swerved savagely across the empty sodden street. 'Tregowan, sir?'

'Yes. Why – is it haunted, or something?' The driver steadied his course, said nothing while he blew his horn at a tabby cat.

'No, sir, not as I've 'eard. But that's where the big boss lives, sir. Foreigner, 'e is.'

'Foreigner?'

'Yessir. Canadian. A General, too: boss o' the 'ole bag o' tricks, 'e is. Perhaps you got the name wrong, sir?'

'No. That'll be the one.' The driver made no further comment: he was wondering how to explain all this to his wife. There would have to be a good reason for a young Naval fellow taking all his bags and such to Tregowan, and the driver's wife was satisfied only with the fullest details. The taxi rattled along the narrow streets, under the grim, Victorian house-fronts, an absorbed and worried man at the wheel.

'Shall I drive in, sir?'

'If there's room. You're right: it is quiet, up here.'

'Ah. Quiet as the grave.' The gateposts drew slowly past, as though the taxi, or its driver, or both, were unwilling to enter the domain of so exalted a foreigner.

'You wouldn't be a Canadian, now, would you, sir?'

'No, I'm English. But my mother's married to a Canadian. The General.' The driver expelled a long breath. So that was it. One more of the town girls got swept off her feet. There'd be a pretty to-do when the lads came back: he had often said so. Not that they were bad chaps, these Canadians: only a bit queer, being from foreign parts.

' 'Ere's y' bags, sir. Four shillings.'

'Five to you?'

'Thank ye, sir. But I can see you ain't no Canadian. I'd get more 'n that, from a Canadian.'

'Perhaps they get paid more.'

'They do that. And y' see, sir, I've 'eard as 'ow there ain't nothing in Canada for 'em to spend money on. So of course, when they gets to Ambershott, well!' The old man spread out his hands: what did you expect? I 'ope you'll like it 'ere, sir. Better ring the bell.

'Thanks. I will.' But he waited until the taxi had trundled itself backwards out through the gates: then he rang, heard the ringing deep inside the house. It was half-past nine on a Sunday morning.

It was later on the same day that the Captain took a taxi: he climbed into it at Portsmouth station, paid it off outside the Queens Hotel. When he had unpacked his grip, he went downstairs to the phone box.

Pamela was delighted to hear of his arrival: she was on duty, she told him, all day, but he could pick her up at five at the Wrennery. She'd have to break her date with George Witherton. Arthur said that he didn't think she'd have a date, when they were almost engaged: he meant it as a joke, but Pamela took it seriously, just sighed and said that she'd see him at five.

Rather a silly girl, he thought. But she's fun, when she gets what she wants and nothing is difficult. The Captain had a feeling that she only tolerated Naval Officers because, being a Wren, she found them handy, usually presentable escorts. He had a feeling that she regarded men as something to be made use of: when she wanted one to be nice to her, she was nice to him, but only for a good reason.

Arthur had dropped in to see his mother, in London, before he caught the Portsmouth train. He had been permitted to see her in bed, having breakfast. Mrs Hallet was a self-preserved woman of middle age: she never rose before ten, and began her war-work after lunch. For want of anything better to say, Arthur told her that he was thinking of becoming engaged.

'Ridiculous, Arthur! At your age! Who is she?'

'She's a Wren: Pamela Sainsbury.'

'Sounds like a grocer's daughter. You had better go and shave, Arthur. Was there no hot water in the train?'

He left the phone booth, deciding to spend a little time in the bar, before lunch. It was lonely in the crowd of strangers, and he was beginning to wonder why he had left London, when a couple of friends whom he hadn't seen for years emerged from the throng beside him. Of course, this was Pompey, where you always met your friends.

Friends? Well, acquaintances: brother officers. Not necessarily friends: only one in a hundred came into that category. Most of them you'd known since you were thirteen: by the time you were seventeen and Chief Cadet Captain at Dartmouth, few of them were friends. They were careful to stay on good terms with you: they watched carefully, waiting for you to slip up. Then, perhaps, 'Remember Hallet? He was Chief C.C. You'd never think so, now. Going down the drain, old boy ... Missed getting an operational command.... Got that frightful Southsea slut for a mistress.... Flash in the pan, old boy.'

They couldn't say it yet.

The tankards were empty:

'Three more, please,' he called, and he watched the barmaid as she dragged the handles down: she thought of her permanent wave, and while her hands and wrists moved the handles her bright smile faded and she wondered about whether or not she'd have to lose a tooth the next time she visited the dentist.

The bell pealed again inside the house called Tregowan. It was remote, nothing to do with the bell-push: like the cry of pain that came separately, a little moment after the squeeze on the trigger. Obviously nobody was going to answer the door: the Sub left the porch, walked round to the back door. It was locked, and there was no sound from inside: probably this was where the bell rang when he pressed the button on the front.

The top part of the window was open. It was a small window, and limited in its opening, but there might be room to worm through. The Sub wedged one foot on the curve of the kitchen waste-pipe, curled the fingers of one hand round the edge of the window-frame. He stuck his head and shoulders into the kitchen, leant on the inner sill, slid through. He stood up, dusted down his Number One uniform.

He hoped that this was the right house: things could be a

little awkward otherwise. Even the crash of his entry had caused no sign of life, no voice or footstep. He left the kithen, explored the lower rooms: in the drawing-room were photographs that he knew: there was even one of himself, at the age of sixteen, a Cadet, a small, undamaged face, clean white tabs on the lapels. The ashes of a fire lay in the grate.

Leaving the house through the front door, he carried in his two suitcases, dumped them in the hall before he climbed the stairs, cream-painted stairs, the carpet thick and soft. On the landing, he knew for the first time that the house held life: he heard a snore. It was a deep snore, a pleasant sound. The Sub opened the door, and his mother shrieked.

Not with fear. His mother had never really been frightened in her life. She came of an old Border family that had in its blood the acceptance of surprise. Now, it was with surprise and delight that she shrieked: beside her, in the bed, lay the man she loved, in the doorway the boy she had reared. Her exclamation woke the General, who heaved himself still half asleep into a sitting position in his broadly-striped pyjamas.

'Well!' The big man drawled the word in a pleasantly soft accent. He had a big, friendly face.

'So there we are. You're rushing off to God knows where, and I'm expected to stay here like an old maid for the next five years. The fact that I'm ill doesn't worry you at all, does it?'

'Don't be an idiot.' Harry, the Engineer, looked wearily across at his wife. 'There's a war on: you know I have to go where I'm sent.'

'Is there a war on, Harry? I wouldn't have known. Do you think I'm used to living like this?'

'Like what?'

'Oh, it's all right for you. You come here for a few days and expect to find a loving little wife waiting for you. At least you get about, see people. You've got a job to be interested in. What have I got to think about? You think...'

Shd had the look that said she was about to cry. Harry was sick of tears. There were people who had something to cry about and yet didn't....

'You could join the Wrens again. The doctor says you're fit.'

'Fit? For what? This? Oh, I can't expect you to understand, can I?'

Harry knocked out his pipe. There was little point in trying to answer. He looked quickly round as though he hadn't known where the door was, and as though he was relieved at finding it, the way out.

'I think I'll ring Arthur, at the Queens.'

'At this time of night?'

'Pubs are shut. He'll be just about back. I said I'd ring.' He thought, I'm making excuses, explaining myself now. What happens when there's no war to go to?

'And you imagine that just because the pubs are shut Arthur'll go straight back to his little bed?' The Engineer's wife smiled. 'He's not married yet, you know.'

After a few days at Ambershott, the Sub travelled down to Sussex to stay with the Bishop family. Before his mother married the General, they had always lived there, in Sussex, always known the Bishops. The Bishops were a part of Sussex as rooted as the Downs, as permanent and necessary as the sweep of country that fell clear from the Three Bells to the distant sea. For the Sub, the Bishops were as much a family as his own, particularly when he felt that his mother had a new life of her own to make and that if he married a widow he'd rather not have her children as well.

Major Bishop was known to his friends as Bish. He was a man of late middle age, bald and a little stocky. His heart was in the land that had reared the generations before him, and when the spirits moved him his talk was always of the '14 War, in which, he would state in support of any argument, he had 'Gone over the Top'. Whenever he made that statement, his wife was inclined to start giggling, and his son and daughter were apt to remind him that they had heard it on previous occasions. In the Sub's opinion, there was no family in England more wholly English or more completely united in itself than the family Bishop.

Bish was a busy man, these days. Well over military age, he had enrolled as a part-time worker in a local factory that produced fuel-tanks for aircraft. He had become a foreman: intensely interested, he was ready at any time to describe in detail the production problems of a modern factory. Determined to play a full part in his country's battle, Bish enrolled for night duty as a Special Constable, wearing the helmet and belt with all the confidence of a regular policeman. When he returned home, late in the evening, and laid down these badges of office on the arm of a settee, his family saw the strain in the face of a man who had never played any part smaller than that within his reach.

As the Sub had once said, over a pint of bitter, to a friend in the Ram's Head, Bish was a lovely man. Now, leaning on the oaken bar of that establishment, he listened and watched while Bishop talked to old Todd. Todd was saying that he'd never known a gentleman like Mr Forster, never, God rest his soul.

'H'm. Handy man with a gun, wasn't he?'

''E was that, Major. And I never knew a man wi' such knowledge o' fruit.'

'Fruit, eh?'

'Ah. There's been many a time 'e'd take a seat by that window, and I'd take an apple or a pear, or whatever it might be, out o' me pocket, and 'e'd look at un, an' maybe 'e'd take a sniff at un, apple or pear, or whatever it might be, and 'e'd say, "Why," 'e'd say, "that's a so-an'-so apple or pear"; or whatever it might be. Never known 'im wrong, Major, never.'

Later, walking slowly home, the Sub said:

'You know, Bish, I reckon that men who love the land and men who love the sea have a lot in common. The same sort of love: the same faith, if you like.'

'Daresay you're right, boy.' Bish looked faintly surprised. Next thing you knew, the boy'd be writing to the papers.

The Sussex evening and the quiet, homely friendship: here, awake and in daylight, he was dreaming again. He was dreaming that this belonged to him, that he belonged here, that roots existed for him as much as they did for the Bishops. He remembered a school report that had worried his mother: it said, 'John lives in a world of his own...'

It was easier to dream, to see things as he wanted them to be. He could even imagine, for instance, that his father had also been worried by that report. In his heart, the Sub knew that his father had never had any lasting interest in his youngest son, the product of his second marriage. His father lived in the past, among friends who were already, most of them, dead. They were not dead to the Sub's father: they lived as hard as they had always done, riding hard, drinking hard, living in the only way that they had ever wanted to live. Only the Sub's father was condemned to go on living for ten years longer, alone with the past, in a seaside villa with a single yapping terrier and a young family with whom he had nothing in common.

Once he had told them, 'I want to live long enough to see my son in uniform.'

Strange, thought the Sub, to have been so thrilled at such a remark! When he heard it, he had felt as though he had been given an unexpected, needed present, his father's interest. It was the first and only sign of it that he had ever seen. Not that he missed consciously something that he had never held: only that a taste, a flashing glimpse, filled him with longing.

Now, at the age of twenty, the Sub expected no warmth in human relationships. Rather he shunned it, telling himself that it was sentiment, womanly, unbecoming in a man. He had no close ties, now that his mother was making her own life: good luck to her!

The future? Dreams took the place of the future, dreams and a lack of thought. The future held nothing of interest, only the past held whispers of promise. In his mind there was no idea of what he wanted in the years ahead. But then, in war-time, people were killed. Knowing that he looked forward to nothing, the Sub sometimes wondered whether that would not, perhaps, be a logical conclusion.

The Captain, the Engineer and the Navigator sit round the wardroom table, having breakfast. The First Lieutenant is on watch in the Control Room, and the hiss that comes frequently from that direction as the periscope is raised and lowered tells its own story of a careful watch. The Sub, who was relieved of the watch an hour and a half ago, at six o'clock, is asleep in his bunk.

'Better shake John, Chief,' suggests the Navigator. 'Won't be anything left to eat.' Chief reaches behind him and bangs his fist on the figure in the bunk, and Sub heaves himself up on one elbow and stares moodily at the scene. Smelling sausages he feels better, swings his legs out and eases himself straight on to the locker which serves as a seat for two men.

'Morning,' he says, his eyes half open and looking for food.

'My God!' murmurs Chief, looking at him sympathetically.

'What's the matter with you?'

'I've heard the expression "death dug up",' answers Chief, sipping his coffee, 'and I've seen things crawl out of heaps of muck in wet gardens, but – did you sleep well, Sub?'

'Very amusing. Wilkins – coffee, please!' Able Seaman Wilkins brings it in and sets it down.

'Morning, sir. Bangers?'

'Yes, please. Did you eat yours, Chief?'

'No, I did not.'

'I'll have the Engineer Officer's too, please.'

'Sorry, Sub,' puts in the Captain. 'I had them.'

'H'm. Wilkins!'

'Sir?'

'Have you reloaded the other two Oerlikon magazines?'

'Yes, sir.' Apart from being Wardroom Messman, Wilkins is also the Oerlikon Gunner.

Breakfast is finished and cleared away, and Sub turns in again. It is very warm and quiet, an atmosphere full of sleep for the men off watch as the submarine motors slowly along at periscope depth, thirty feet on the depth-gauges. The Captain climbs into his bunk and closes his eyes. Then he opens them again and presses the Control Room buzzer. A messenger appears.

'Sir?'

'Ask the First Lieutenant to see me.' The Captain stares at the wardroom lamp while he hears Number One send the periscope down before reporting.

'Yes, sir?'

'Let me know if you see any fishing-boats big enough to hold

34

the Chinks we've got.'

'Aye aye, sir.' Number One moves back into the Control Room, and they hear him say 'Up periscope', the hiss and thump as it rises and stops. There is a loud cough, and Chief looks up to see Engineroom Artificer Featherstone drooping in the gangway.

'Want me, Featherstone?'

Featherstone regards him sourly. 'Them flippin' 'eads is flipped,' he announces. The Captain rolls over on his bunk.

'What, again?'

'Yessir. I'd like to catch the bugger that keeps flippin' 'em up, sir. Spend 'alf me time off watch putting 'em right and before I got time to put me flippin' tools away the bloody door's open an' shut a couple o' times and the bastard's floodin' up and jammed!'

The Engineer Officer sticks his dirty feet into a pair of sandals that should have been thrown away a long time ago. 'Let's see what's wrong,' he suggests.

'I know what's wrong.' Featherstone's off again. 'Some bugger goes in 'ere an' does 'is bit an' leaves the flippin' valve open. Or 'e tries to blow 'em with the valve flippin' well shut.'

In a few moments, Chief comes back. 'He's quite right, you know. It's time you people learnt to use the heads. Every damn day of your lives you go in there, and someone hasn't got the guts to ask what he's doing wrong.'

'Grumpy old bastard. If the heads didn't go wrong occasionally your department 'd have nothing to do. And it's you that wrecks them, as likely as not. Shouldn't eat so much.'

'Young man, I was blowing submarine heads before you were bloody well born!'

'Before I was born there wasn't any such things in submarines. I've read about it. When they surfaced at night, chaps sat over the side of the bridge with someone hanging on to their feet.'

Tommy, the Navigator, grins at the cork-painted deckhead over his bunk. 'That reminds me,' he says, 'of the story about the sailor in Chatham dockyard who —'

'Shut up!' barks the Captain. 'I want some sleep.'

Twenty minutes is all he gets, because Tommy has only been

35

on watch in the Control Room for five minutes, having taken over from Number One, before he sights a fair-sized fishing-boat. The messenger shakes the Captain, who tumbles out of his bunk, takes a quick look and orders: 'Diving Stations. Chinese passengers stand by in the Control Room.'

The submarine is on the surface for about two minutes, during which time the Chinese are hurried into the fishing-boat and the only occupant of that craft is supplied with an outsize tin of corned beef and a tin-opener. It is probably the most solid food the man has seen for years, and his puzzled expression is tinged with pleasurable anticipation as the submarine sinks slowly from his sight. Through the periscope from thirty feet the Captain is amused to watch introductions and explanations taking place in the fishing-boat, which is overcrowded enough without the owner and his guests having to bow to each other from precarious positions around the gunwales.

The Sub leant down to the voice-pipe and shouted:
'Control Room!'
'Control Room,' answered the helmsman.
'Tell the Captain: land in sight, red three-oh to red ten.'
Low on the port bow lay part of the East coast of Ceylon. Trincomali, the base from which the submarine flotilla operated, lay right ahead. Three and a half days ago, *Seahound* had left the Straits: this evening, she'd be secured alongside her Depot Ship.

The Captain, wearing only a pair of khaki shorts, arrived on the bridge and turned his glasses on to the hazy, cloud-like line of coast that would soon resolve itself into dark-green forests edged with white sand and an even whiter line of surf.

'Dead on,' he commented. 'I suppose you'll all disgrace me again, tonight?'

'Early night for me, sir.'

'One day, Sub, I daresay someone'll get back from patrol and turn in early. But not before the Socialists or the Yanks have deprived us of our liquor.'

'Think the Socialists have a chance of getting in, sir?'

'A lot of people seem to think so. Get a bearing of the edge, when you can see it.'

'Aye aye, sir.'

In the Control Room, the Signalman was sitting with the Jolly Roger in his lap, sewing on the marks of a successful patrol. A group of men stood around, getting in the light and impeding his efforts with suggestions and advice. The Torpedo Gunner's Mate, Chief Petty Officer Rawlinson, looked down at the flag with evident displeasure. 'This ain't a submarine. It's a ruddy gunboat.'

The Captain stops at the bottom of the ladder.

'Cheer up, Rawlinson. We may use some fish, yet.'

'What on, sir? Junks?'

'There's always hope of meeting something worthwhile, before we finish.' The First Lieutenant came for'ard, from the Motor Room.

'Number One: we'll be in about five. Better get cracking on the brass.'

'Aye aye, sir. Cox'n in the Control Room.' A messenger went for the Cox'n.

'Yessir!'

'Turn some hands to up top, on the brasswork. Gun's Crew off watch on the gun.'

'Aye aye, sir.' The Cox'n went shambling for'ard, roaring names as he passed from compartment to compartment.

On patrol the going is rough. It is not considered necessary to shave, and it is not possible to have a bath: moreover, fresh water is precious and must be conserved in order that the patrol can last several weeks and there may still be something to drink. Excessive washing is not encouraged. At the end of a patrol, however, the submarine and her men have to look smart when they enter harbour, as smart as any other ship which may have been swinging round a buoy in that harbour for weeks. So the bright-work is polished, jowls are shaved, and there is a queue for the use of the washbasins. Each man has a spotless set of white uniform, carefully stowed out of the way of dirt all through the patrol, kept inside-out for greater safety, so that when the time comes to enter harbour with the eyes of the fleet upon them every man will look what he is, a seaman, and what is more, a seaman in the Royal Navy. It is a form of pride, a pride well nurtured and now a tradition. And proud *Seahound* looked as she swept through the gap in the boom, her Ensign fluttering wildly and the heavier black flag flapping more lazily from a slightly raised periscope. The casing was lined fore-and-aft by seamen standing properly at ease as they would on a parade ground: the brass in the bridge, the brass rail round it and the bright-work of the gun gleamed golden in the evening sun as the submarine reduced speed and approached the Depot Ship whose decks were crowded with her own men and with the crews of the submarines in harbour.

Passing the Depot Ship's stern. Number One ordered 'Pipe!' and the Signalman, standing at the after end of the bridge, sounded the 'Still', a high, clear note on a Bosun's Call: at the same time the men on the casing were called to attention as the Captain faced the Depot Ship and saluted. Loud and clear over the harbour, a bugle-call from the big ship's quarter-deck answered the salute.

His Majesty's Submarine *Seahound* was home from another patrol.

Arthur Hallet, the C.O., came out of his cabin in the Depot Ship, tightening the cummerbund that served two purposes. First, it kept his trousers up: second, it served as an essential part of Red Sea Rig, the compulsory dress for officers at dinner. White open-necked shirt with epaulettes, black trousers, black cummerbund. It was a smart rig, cool and comfortable as well.

He turned out of the cabin flat, stopped to look down over the side, a bird's-eye view of the submarine alongside. *Seahound*, just returned, was outside the two other submarines on this side: in the morning there would be a reshuffle, the two inside would lie off to let *Seahound* reberth alongside the Depot Ship, so that the cranes and derricks could plumb her hatches, haul out the torpedoes due for overhaul in the big ship's workshops.

There was pride in his eyes as he looked down at his ship. Another patrol finished, some more of the enemy destroyed, his ship and his men brought safely back. It wasn't chance that turned a lot of apparatus and a bunch of widely-assorted men into an efficient submarine. He remembered his first impressions of this new command. A cold, autumn morning in Scotland, a dirty submarine in a grey dock: he had met his officers in the base, ashore, and the meeting had hardly been reassuring. He found he had a First Lieutenant who regarded him with suspicion and distrust. He found a Navigator who could probably be relied upon to do his job but who was too quiet and colourless to lend much influence on the character of the ship itself. The Engineer Officer's attitude was decidedly hostile, and the Torpedo Officer was a young Dartmouth Sub-Lieutenant who happened, at the time of their meeting, to be under arrest.

Hallet saw that the Engineer was the worst of the lot, and he decided, within a minute of shaking the man's hand, that this particular Engineer would not sail East in *Seahound*. Not if he could help it. The combination of familiarity and subservience was vaguely sickening. This was an officer who would try to be popular with the men at the expense of the officers, popular with the officers at the expense of the men. Privately, Arthur would have described him as a tyke.

He knew the reason for his First Lieutenant's distrust. He knew how young Commanding Officers were regarded by experienced yet less successful submariners. They called them 'Boy C.O.'s'. They were assumed to have got where they were by pushing, by always saying the right thing to the right people. Arthur had an idea that in any walk of life young men who went rapidly to the top would be regarded in much the same way. He understood: he'd feel the same way himself if he were still a First Lieutenant and one of his immediate contemporaries were his C.O. He had no worries about this First Lieutenant, though: he knew the man's record, and he knew that by the time they left for the East the distrust would be gone. If he had been what the term 'Boy C.O.' suggested, perhaps he would have returned the distrust with dislike: as it was, he left it for the next few months to dissolve.

The Sub was rather a problem. The youngster had done a few patrols, and his record from those patrols was good. The other part of his record was not so striking: as a Midshipman in surface ships he had been regarded as insubordinate and lazy. On his Sub-Lieutenant's courses, young Ferris didn't bear thinking about. Now, he was under arrest. He'd have to see the Captain of the Submarine Flotilla in the morning. The story, as Arthur had heard it, was that Ferris and two other young officers had drunk too much on the evening before, that Ferris had produced a ·38 revolver of which he was illegally in possession. and that they had hung fire-buckets from the garden railings of the Junior Officers' Hostel and blown holes in the buckets from a distance of twenty yards. The bullets that missed had fallen in the dockyard around a destroyer's gangway, and sailors returning from shore-leave had been forced to take cover. The Officer-of-the-day had sent his messenger down to put a stop to the shooting, and the messenger had been sent back with a message to the effect that the officers were only having target-practice. It was after midnight, and the officers had then been placed under arrest.

After dinner in the Mess, Arthur Hallet sent for Ferris. The youngster stood to attention, just inside the door of his C.O.'s cabin.

'Well, sir, that's the whole story. I didn't think we were doing any harm: that was why I sent that message back, sir. But I'm sorry about the street lights.'

'Street lights?'

'Didn't you know about them, sir?' There was only honesty in the boy's face.

'Oh, yes, the street lights. But don't mention them tomorrow morning.' So the young idiots hadn't been satisfied with fire-buckets. 'Look, Ferris. I think you've been drinking too much lately.'

'Yes, sir.'

'Have you?'

'Yes, sir.'

'Well, the least you can expect is to have your wine-bill and your leave stopped. Will you give me your word in any case to stop drinking for three months?'

'Yes, sir.'

'Your record at sea, Ferris, is passable. Your record ashore is disgraceful. In my ship I won't have my officers behaving like hooligans. The war's nearly over now, Ferris: there aren't many operational flotillas left. There are hundreds of young officers

40

who'd fall over themselves to take your place in *Seahound*. When *Seahound* leaves for the Far East, she'll have only good officers in her. Do you understand?'

'Perfectly, sir.'

'Very well. I'll see the Captain in the morning, before you do. Carry on, please.' John Ferris wheeled about, returned to his quarters. At ten-thirty next morning he was given the dressing-down of his life: he was also given three months' drink stopped and three months' leave stopped. The offence and the punishment were to be recorded in the ship's logbook.

After that incident, the Sub became a model of good behaviour: sooner than leave *Seahound*, he'd have shot himself. Score One, thought the Captain, as he leaned on the rail and thought of the early days of the commission.

During the 'work-up' period, the months which they spent practising every possible evolution, the weather was no help: off the Scottish coast the gales were as they are reported every year, the worst for forty years. Arthur Hallet remembered bringing his ship up alongside a destroyer in Larne, the little Irish port, the rain lashing horizontally, the wind a tearing force that could easily have blown the whole casing party off the casing if they hadn't the sense to hang on with one hand while they worked with the other at the ropes and wires: heave in, surge, check, keep it out of the water – Number One shouted himself hoarse through a brass megaphone at the men who toiled with frozen fingers on the wave-lashed casing. Seeing that help was needed aft, Number One climbed down and joined them. He'd seen his C.O. do a first-class job in bringing *Seahound* alongside, and there had been several months of the same sort of impressions. When he rejoined the Captain on the bridge, there was confidence and respect in place of suspicion and distrust. The Captain thought, Score Two.

He heard, while they were in Larne, that the Engineer was giving a birthday party ashore. That evening he found that Sub was Duty Officer.

'Evening, Sub. Sorry you're missing Chief's party.'

'I'm not worried, sir.' Next day, the Sub went into the engine-room to hang up some wet clothes to dry. They'd been at sea all day, under the usual conditions. The Leading Stoker asked,

41

'Why wasn't you with us ashore, sir, last night? Proper do, we 'ad.'

'I was Duty, Williams, or I'd have been there.'

'No you wouldn't 've, m'lad. It was my birthday party, see, and I don't ask young Dartmouth twirps when I have a party!' It was the Engineer. The group of Stokers looked embarrassed. So was the Engineer, when he turned and saw the Captain on the steel step. Later, the Captain called the Engineer aside.

'Brown,' he said, 'that was the first time in my life that I have heard one officer deliberately insult another in the presence of ratings. Is that sort of thing a habit of yours?'

'I don't see that kid as an officer. He's hardly weaned, and he thinks he's some sort of bloody Admiral.'

'That's neither here nor there. This is one of His Majesty's Ships, and I'll not have an Engineer Officer in her who behaves like a hard case in the stokehold of a Panamanian tramp. What are you going to do about it, Brown?'

'I do my job, sir.'

'About half of it. I'm taking a happy ship away when we leave, Brown. I don't think you fit in.'

'Suits me, sir.'

'Very good. I'll ask for a relief for you when we get in.' Score Three. And that was the hardest part over and done with. Now he could get on with the job in a better atmosphere. But other troubles came along, too. There was a theft, and a man charged, punishment by Warrant. There was a call at a small Scottish port where a bunch of seamen got themselves mixed up in a dance-hall fight: someone was hurt, a knife wound, and the dance-hall people blamed one of the Seahounds. The Sub was Duty Officer when a Lieutenant from the shore base rang through on the telephone, told him to send a patrol to the dance-hall.

'Sorry,' replied the Sub. 'I have only the Duty Watch on board, and I can't let any of them go.'

'I'm giving you an order.'

'I am acting under the orders of my Commanding Officer.'

'Do you realize that men from your ship are tearing the place apart, you young fool?'

The Sub didn't like being called names by strange, shore-based officers. 'I think that's extremely unlikely,' he answered.

The Captain, returning later, backed him up. But as a result they were forbidden to enter the port: on subsequent exercises, they anchored outside. Arthur Hallet smiled when he heard the Signalman remark, 'Thank God f' that. 'Oo'd want to spend a night in that 'orrible little 'ole?' Where they lay at anchor, it was blowing a gale. That same night, over a bottle of whisky, the Captain told Number One the story of how he had lost a year's seniority once, by striking a policeman in Malta. It was the sort of story he had not been able to tell before, when he was regarded as a pusher, as a man who had got on by always being a good boy.

The gale increased, and *Seahound* dragged anchor: while they were moving her to a more sheltered berth, the freezing wind was warmed by the language thrown against it. There was a healthy spirit among the smells of shale oil and wet clothes, the talk of leave and the eagerness to sail and join their flotilla.

The Captain remembered the relief that he had felt at that time: now, looking down on his submarine from the Depot Ship's rail, he knew that he commanded a ship as happy and as efficient as any that floated.

He lit a cigarette, turned and headed towards the Wardroom. As he appeared, the Captain of another submarine hailed him.

'Be with you in a moment, Barney.' Arthur Hallet crossed the room, joined his First Lieutenant who had a drink already poured for him.

CHAPTER TWO

The Sub and the Navigator lived not in the Depot Ship itself but in another large ship, an old passenger liner which lay at anchor close by and was used as an accommodation ship for some of the crews and for junior officers. As far as the junior officers were concerned this was a very satisfactory arrangement, since with only junior officers using the Mess, life was considerably less formal than in the Wardroom of the Depot Ship.

Certainly there is nothing formal about the game called Bok-Bok. This game had been introduced to the flotilla by a group of South African officers, and since the first introduction it had remained a firm favourite amongst after-dinner recreations. Two teams are drawn, the leaders choosing them with an eye to weight and stamina. A toss decides which team goes first to the wall, where they form a line, crouching one behind the other, each man's head between the legs of the man in front of him. Hang on with your arms, bind tight like a rugger scrum and wait for Jannie van Rensburg to come down like a ton of bricks on top of you. They come rapidly, the other team, one after the other, leaping high in the air in order to land as heavily as possible on the enemy line. If you've been the man under Jannie van Rensburg, you will not be expected to take part in the following bout.

At about midnight everyone stripped and dived over the side to cool off, another thing that was not allowed in the Depot Ship, where senior officers were present to enforce the regulations. It felt good, to get some exhausting exercise after three weeks patrol.

It was funny to think that people used to pay a lot of money to travel from one place to another in this old ship. If anything there was less room in the cabins than there was in the Wardroom of the submarine, and the place was alive with cock-

44

roaches. Cockroaches have a musty smell all of their own, and their breeding capacity would fill rabbits with envy: getting rid of them had always been a problem. Lying there in his bunk and listening to them nibbling something in the ventilation trunk over his head, the Sub remembered how they had tried to get rid of the pests in the wardroom of a destroyer. They put a full-sized smoke-float in the pantry and the Torpedo Gunner set it off, then rushed on deck and battened down. An hour later he went down to see how things were, vanished into the heavy white smoke and failed to return, so the First Lieutenant, wearing a breathing apparatus, went down and dragged the Gunner out half dead. Eventually the fans cleared the smoke out and there were more cockroaches than ever, big, happy cockroaches in the best of health and with enormous appetites.

Sleep held off, probably a result of the violent exercise of the evening, and the Sub's mind ran over the excitements of the last patrol. The start had been unfortunate, a lesson that whatever you were doing and wherever you were you must keep an eye on the sky, even when you're busy shooting at something on the surface and the shoot is taking all your concentration. They had started a patrol off the Nicobar Islands and the weather was kicking up a bit, the sea rough enough to make it tricky keeping periscope depth without showing too much periscope or even a bit of the bridge. On the second day Number One was on watch in the Control Room, when he sighted one of the two Tank Landing Ships which the enemy used for supplying the Nico-bars and the Andamans. Jimmy's poker-face grew a little redder than usual and he said all in one breath, 'Captain in the Control Room, Diving Stations.' The bored men on watch were suddenly bored no longer: after a day or a week or two on patrol you began to feel that life was rather pointless when no enemy came near and there was no return for the continued discomfort.

'Tank Landing Ship, sir. Red four five.' The Captain took a look and saw at once that there was no chance of getting into position to fire torpedoes. He hoped the enemy's armament didn't amount to too much as he said,

'Stand by Gun Action.'

Up for'ard, the T.I. cursed under his breath and wondered

why they bothered to do routines on tubes and torpedoes when the Japs only went afloat in rowing-boats.

The Gun's Crew were closed up, and behind them the Ammunition Party had the first shells ready on the wardroom deck. The cook's face peered anxiously out through the small aperture from the magazine, where he worked passing up shells during the action. He looked like a rat staring out of a drain-pipe.

The Captain, looking into the periscope, said, 'Target a Tank Landing Ship. Bearing ... that! Range...' he fiddled with a knob on the periscope, 'Range ... that!'

Sub set the angle on another machine and said, 'Seven thousand eight hundred.' His face, he hoped, showed none of the anxiety in his mind. It wouldn't be easy, shooting in this weather.

The Captain spoke again. 'Enemy speed nine. We're on her starboard quarter.'

Sub used the instrument again and reported, 'Deflection two right.' He shouted up the Gun-tower hatch to the Gun's Crew: 'Bearing Red two-oh, range oh-eight-oh, deflection two right, shoot!' The order Shoot meant that as soon as the gun was ready and aimed at the enemy the Gunlayer could fire without having to wait for an order from the bridge. The Layer repeated back the order to show that he understood it.

'Down periscope.... Surface!'

As soon as the submarine broke surface they knew how rough it was: when the Sub climbed out of the hatch into the bridge they were right over to port, swinging over: he saw the crest of a wave before it slapped into the bridge. A second later he was sitting on the front of the bridge, watching through his binoculars for the splash that would mark the fall of their first shot. No splash was sighted, so the shot was repeated with the same settings on the gun and the splash went up left.

'Right eight, shoot!' In line, short.

'Up four hundred, shoot!' The first shot couldn't have been far short: this one was over. 'Down two hundred, shoot!' Short, again. 'Up one hundred, shoot!' A red-orange flash and a puff of smoke on the enemy's bridge, right aft. But that had come too soon to be a hit: it was the enemy firing back. *Seahound*'s shell hit the Jap Landing Ship's stern a few seconds later. That was at least a three-inch they were shooting back with from the gun-deck just abaft the bridge: it had to be knocked out, that gun. The submarine was rolling like a drunkard and her next shot missed, while the enemy fired again and the splash was plain to see a cable's length on *Seahound*'s quarter. It was hell's own job trying to shoot at this range on a platform that was about as steady as a bucking horse, but the submarine scored one more hit out of three more shots before the Captain yelled 'Down Below!'

That meant an emergency, no time for securing the gun, no time for anything but getting down below like split lightning: the submarine would be on her way down before the hatch was shut, what American films call a 'Crash Dive'. Sub blew his whistle, a long hard blast that sent the Gun's Crew leaping for the hatch, leaving the gun aimed out over the port bow with the smoking breech still open. As the Gun-tower hatch clanged down, Sub jumped for the bridge hatch, dropping through on top of Wilkins, the Oerlikon Gunner, who wasn't quite fast enough to avoid injury. As he dropped through, Sub looked up and saw the reason for the hurry: a Jap bomber with its nose down coming out of the sky like a rocket.

The next minute passed like half-an-hour, waiting for the bomb, but when the boat was steady at sixty feet the tense looks eased off and expressions of angry frustration took their place. The Captain muttered, 'Stay at sixty feet, Number One....' He turned away, rubbing the side of his chin with the back of his left hand, and he added, 'I'd like to meet that bugger again, one day.'

Perhaps they would, thought the Sub, dreamily. He was dropping off to sleep, and as he dropped off there was a smile on his face: in forty-eight hours' time, he'd be on leave, he'd be in Kandy. He'd see Sheila.

Carrying his suitcase, the Sub walked from the café in Kandy's main street, where the lorry had discharged its passengers, up and around the corner towards the Queens Hotel. The Queens was one of those places, like the Cecil in Alexandria, the Mount Nelson in Cape Town or the Four Seasons in

Hamburg, that nobody who visits the country can help having something to do with. In Kandy, no officer had ever been known to stay anywhere else, except perhaps out of town at a planter's house. The reputed disadvantage of staying at a planter's house was the overwhelming hospitality of some planters: an officer who returned from leave with the symptoms of *delirium tremens* was likely to be frowned upon.

The Sub handed his case to the hall porter, and leant over the reception desk.

'Ferris. I sent you a wire.'

'Yes, Mr Ferris.' The Singhalese clerk pushed the book across the marble counter, and handed a key to the porter. 'Number thirteen.'

'Hell! Do I have to have thirteen?'

'You are superstitious, sir? It is the room you occupied when you were last here in Kandy.'

'Not particularly superstitious,' the Sub answered as he turned away. 'But it certainly failed to bring me any startling success, last time.' Sheila's green eyes were all over the place as he followed the porter through the foyer and acknowledged a minor salaam from the bar-boy. The bar-boy had an easy life: his customers supplied their own liquor, and, in return for the iced water or minerals that he produced, tipped him as though his services were of the usual value.

The porter deposited his burden on the huge bed, which, festooned with mosquito nets, still occupied only a small part of the room. The Sub tipped him, then emptied his case and rang the bell.

'Master?' A little brown man bowed himself in, grinning happily.

'I want these things pressed, and my half-boots cleaned.'

'Yes, master.' The little man pattered round, picking things up. 'Master want bath?'

'Yes, please. At six.' He put all the bottles back in his case, and locked it, slipped a flask into his pocket and strolled down to the lounge.

'A glass, please, and some iced water.' He lit a cigarette, and relaxed. A couple of gins in a comfortable chair, and the lorry stiffness was wearing off. He crossed over to the telephone box, and rang Sheila's number. She was out: Missy had gone into town with her mother. He went back to his table, poured out a little more gin and lit another cigarette. The place was almost empty. At one table two majors stared glassily at each other, trying perhaps to match the vacancy on each others' faces, while at another a young captain and a plump, motherly Wren were engaged in small-talk. The Sub finished his drink, stubbed out his cigarette and headed for the doors.

The music and the wine were finished: Kandy, moonlit, was a place of beauty. Hoping that Sheila would say no, the Sub asked her,

'Shall I try to find a taxi?'

'I'd rather walk. It's so lovely at this time, so cool.'

They walked slowly up the deserted road and along beside the low wall that encircled the lake.

'Did you know that the lake is supposed to claim three lives a year?'

'No. Does it run true to form?' He tossed a glowing cigarette end into the water.

'It does. Children, drunks or people just found dead and nobody knows how. It's not very deep.'

Their footsteps were the only sounds in the warm scented night. This place has always been here, he thought. When I was in Sussex, or at school, every night the Sacred Lake was shining and the priests in their yellow robes were hurrying past to the Temple of the Tooth. When dogs were barking in the quiet English night, those drums were throbbing, here in Kandy. Years will pass, and perhaps one day I'll be here again, fighting another war, and although I'll be much older and quite different, this lake will be exactly the same and I'll look at it and think, I was here before, once, and the things that seem important now will be dead and forgotten. Sheila will be old and changed, married to a planter, playing bridge four times a week, and people will say, 'Sheila Watson was quite lovely when she was young. You'd never think it now, would you?'

'What the hell's it all for?' He spoke as much to himself as to her, and she had no answer; only the lake told him, Nothing, it just goes on, and on, because that's the way God made it. And we, he thought, Sheila and I, are about as important and necessary as a couple of ants.

They came to the house, turned in through the gates between the flanking trees. A little way up on the right was a small secluded lawn, palms surrounding it with the tips of their graceful branches almost meeting overhead.

'Let's sit.' She sat down beside him and he took her in his arms, her body warm and supple, her breathing sweetly close to his, the scent of her skin more lovely than that of the night.

'John: we...' The palms bowed low and the lawn rocked, the stars were singing and the world had burst into flames, white flames, when she said, urgently, 'John – look!' All around the little lawn sat small, brown people. Sheila whispered. 'The gardener and his family. That's their hut, behind us.'

The brown people sat cross-legged with their hands folded in their laps. Motionless, silent, they watched the couple in the centre. The Sub stood up, helped Sheila to her feet.

'Is this some ancient form of Singhalese hospitality?'

She answered, quickly, not looking at him, 'It's late, John. I must go in. Good-night.' She moved away, then stopped to add, 'It was a lovely evening.' This was a stranger to whom he said good-night, and it was anger and bewilderment that made him stumble as he hurried down the drive.

He had been silly, he thought. He had put all his trust in a human relationship. Quite properly, naturally, the thing had mis-fired. He wouldn't let himself down like that again.

He had not only wanted Sheila as a mistress. He had wanted her to love him. He had wanted to have her sharing with him, intimately and secretly, something warm and personal.

I've been a fool, he thought: soft! For years I've needed no help, no sympathy. Now I've thrown myself open, and it hurts.

It wouldn't happen again.

Seahound was the inside submarine in the 'trot' of three that lay on the Depot Ship's starboard side. A long gangway ran down from the Depot Ship's well-deck, and narrow planks bridged from the casing of each submarine to the next.

Seahound was embarking ammunition, several hundred rounds, some three-inch High Explosive and some Semi-Armour-Piercing, the latter easily distinguished by their long pointed noses. Most of the crew were employed in this task, standing in a long snake of men down the gangway and over the plank, along the casing up to the for'ard hatch. On the well-deck of the Depot Ship the shells were taken out of their boxes and passed down the line, hand to hand, until they were stacked in the for'ard compartment of the submarine. The Gunlayer worked down in the tiny magazine, which was as hot and as big as an oven, stowing shells in their racks and fitting in the wooden battens between each layer. Occasionally he shouted 'O.K., 'Oppy!' and Hopkins the Trainer began to pass down more shells until he was told to stop. As Hopkins called for them, a couple of seamen brought more shells aft from the hatch.

Up for'ard, clear of the stream of shells, Rawlinson and Shadwell were checking their torpedo stores. In the Petty Officers' Mess, the Cox'n was filling in a form about rum. In the wardroom, the Captain was talking to the First Lieutenant, the Navigator was sorting out copies of Notices to Mariners and the Sub-Lieutenant was going over a file of correspondence. In the Engine-room, the Engineer Officer lay flat on his back, oil-stained, staring up at a large slice of trouble in the port diesel.

It was as hot as hell.

A telegraphist eased himself down the ladder from the Depot Ship, getting in the way of the flow of ammunition.

''Ere: 'oo the 'ell are you shovin'?'

'You're not the only bastard with something to do. I got to get down to the flippin' boat, see?'

'Stupid flippin' son of an oar! Choose yer time, don't yer?'

'Come on, Sparky, out of the flippin' way, or I'll do yer!'

'Takes two to do that sort of thing,' remarked the telegraphist, as he narrowly avoided a serious accident.

'Why, I'd flippin' well rape yer!'

'You and 'oo else? Out o' me way, you beast o' burden.'

A warrant officer, the belt of his khaki shorts supporting his stomach as well as the shorts, appeared on the top of the gangway.

'That's the lot!' he bellowed.

'Thank Christ for that,' grunted a stoker who objected to having been drafted into a seaman's work for the forenoon.

'Why, dear?' asked Bird, in a high, pansy voice. 'Are you feelin' faint?'

Next day, the line of men took their places again on the gangway, only this time it was provisions that they handled: meat, vegetables, bread, tins of sausages, butter, canned fruit, tinned soup, bacon, bags of sugar and flour, boxes of eggs, these and many other things passed down the line, to be checked and stowed away under the Cox's careful supervision.

On the same day *Seahound* took in fresh water and fuel, and that night while the diesels growled steadily away, charging the batteries, most of the ship's company were writing letters home, letters that would be in England in a fortnight's time: where they themselves would be in a fortnight's time, none of them had the slightest idea.

CHAPTER THREE

Sub climbed up into the bridge and saluted the Captain.

'Casing secured, sir,' he reported.

'Very good. Number One?'

'Sir?' The first Lieutenant stepped up from the back of the bridge.

'You can open up for diving. I'll have a word over the Tannoy when I come down.'

'Aye aye, sir.'

Once again, Trincomali was astern, and getting farther away every minute. The same question was in every mind: Which area had they been given this time? Ten minutes later the Captain switched on the microphone in the Control Room, and the question was answered.

'The Fourteenth Army are expected to take Rangoon within the next week. Nobody knows if the Japanese will try to get any men out by sea, but in case they do we'll be waiting for them.

'It's likely that we'll shift our billet after a few days, because it'll soon be obvious whether or not there's going to be an evacuation, and if there isn't we'll be sent elsewhere. If there is, it ought to be short and sharp. Two other submarines, *Setter* and *Slayer*, are already there, a bit higher up than we'll be.

'That's all. Carry on.'

'Go to Patrol Routine when you're ready, Number One.'

'Aye aye, sir.'

The Captain walked forward to the Chart table, where the Navigator was already busy.

That evening the wind rose suddenly, as the barometer had promised, and for the first time in three patrols the submarine was rolling and pitching. Chief looked paler than usual as he pretended to eat his supper.

'I hope to God,' he muttered, 'that it's not going to be like this for three bloody weeks.'

'Not feeling so good, Chief?'

'You shut up.'

'This, no doubt,' murmured Number One, 'is the good-humoured, cheerful, comradely spirit which the books say is essential in the close confines of a submarine.'

'Not of a submarine. It's something in the close confines of Chiefy's tum-tum.'

'What time, Sub, do you go on watch?' Chief eyed the Sub-Lieutenant malevolently as he asked the question.

'In ten minutes.'

'And next after that?'

'Two o'clock. Why?'

'When I hear you shaken, I'll lean out of my bunk and scream with laughter.'

'O.K. I'll hold a basin for you.' Sub wasn't feeling any too good himself, but he knew that all would be well as soon as he got up in the fresh air. There were only two places to be, in bad weather: either on the bridge, or flat on your bunk. When it was really bad, even the bunk was inclined to be unsatisfactory, but there was one position, on your side with your knees up and your feet jammed against the bulkhead, that was better than any. You gradually found out these little things that took the strain off life, or at any rate off your stomach.

He looked at the chart and noted the run that would be covered in his watch, while the others slept down here and he was alone with the wind and the flying sea, along on the front of the bridge which was really only a platform sixteen feet above the level of the sea, when it was calm. When the sea was rough it was often much less than sixteen feet away, and the platform had brass-bound holes in it as well, to let the water out when the submarine surfaced, so that a watch in bad weather was inclined to be a wet two hours. The sea came over the front, sometimes just spray but sometimes solid green water, hard and heavy, and it was as much like riding a surf-board as keeping a watch in a ship of war.

More than a ship of war, though: a weapon, as deadly as any in use, designed for the one purpose of destruction. Standing on the bridge and looking down on the gleaming black hull as it thrashes through the leaping waves you see it as it is, so lethal and sinister that to you it looks as beautiful as anything afloat. The sharp shark's bow leads out from where the casing looks broader, where the hydroplane guards stand dripping, like the head of a snake, venomous and lovely, most certainly alive.

A straight course, no lights from which to fix the ship's position, very little likelihood of anything like an enemy being anywhere near. Only the wind and the sea, the routine of lookouts being relieved, the helmsmen changing over.

'Bridge!'

'Bridge,' you answer, into the voice-pipe.

'Helmsman relieved, sir. Course oh-eight-eight, three-eight-oh revolutions, running charge port.'

'Very good.'

The sea sweeps past, over and under.

'Bridge!'

'Bridge.'

'Relieve lookout, sir?'

'Yes, please.' A moment later a dark figure emerges from the hatch behind you, looks round for a moment and takes over from the man at the back of the bridge. Two minutes pass, and the relieved lookout stands at your shoulder.

'Lookout relieved, sir. Nothing in sight.'

'Right, Rivers.'

'G'night, sir.'

'Good-night.'

In the bottom of the main ballast tanks are open holes. The water stays out because it is met by an equal pressure of air from the inside. The air is kept in because the vents at the top of the tanks are shut, only opened when it is necessary to flood the tanks to dive the submarine. In rough weather, however, some of the air escapes, and to keep the submarine as high up in the water as possible it is necessary from time to time to build up the pressure of air in the tanks.

'Control Room!'

'Control Room.'

'Open all L.P. master blows.'

'Open all L.P. master blows, sir.'

Half a minute later, 'Bridge!'

'Bridge.'

'One, two, three, four and five L.P. master blows open, sir.'

'Start the blower.'

'Start the blower, sir.'

The stokers dislike this procedure. The blower is situated in the after compartment, where they sleep, and it makes a noise.

'Control Room. Tell me when five minutes are up.'

'Aye aye, sir, five minutes.'

The time passes slowly in the great empty circle of the horizon.

'Bridge! – five minutes, sir.'

'Stop the blower, shut all L.P. master blows.'

'Stop the blower, sir. Shut all L.P. master blows.'

Down below they carry out the order.

'Bridge!'

'Bridge.'

'Blower stopped, sir, all L.P. master blows shut.'

'Very good. Shake the First Lieutenant.'

In ten minutes' time Jimmy will be up to take over, and you can get down that ladder, take your wet clothes off and sleep for four hours. There should be no interruptions, tonight or tomorrow night.

Jimmy, the First Lieutenant, looks down on the straight, strong bow, and sees the life in the man-made steel as the hard, stinging spray lashes his face. Ships not only live, he thinks, but talk. Ships are the seamen, while we do our best to live up to their standards.

'How does it feel, down there in the warm sea?'

'Fine.'

'Are you handled well?'

'Well enough. Some of you are seamen.'

'What do you know of seamen?'

'Little. They are few, the great ones.'

'Name some.'

'There was Drake, and a queer little man called Nelson. One

56

called Smith, of whom few men have ever heard, was the greatest of them all. Some of the finest, nearest to the greatest, are
not long dead.'

'Name them.'

'They are not long dead. Their names are still a hurt in
human minds. They will never live in history, like the old ones.
The battles are too frequent, and the names too many.'

'So many?'

'You could count them on the fingers of two hands.'

The bow crashes into a cleft in the sea, wiggles and rises fast,
towering higher than the bridge before it falls again.

'Could I ever be numbered amongst them?'

'You?'

'Could I?'

'You would be perhaps, in time.'

'What do you mean by "would be"? Will I, or not? Damn
you for an old cow!'

'Would be.'

'Would be, if what?'

The roar of the sea is the only answer, the roar of the sea and
the way it laughs while it dances.

It is two days later and the Navigator is on watch, on the
surface still, the time five-thirty, in the morning watch. In the
Night Order Book the Captain has ordered, 'Call me at five-
thirty.'

Tommy bends down to the voice-pipe.

'Control room!'

'Control Room.'

'Shake the Captain.'

'Shake the Captain, sir.'

A few minutes later he appears out of the hatch and stares
out over the port bow, where as soon as light comes they expect
to see the Andaman Islands. These islands, once a leper colony,
are now the limit of Japanese expansion in the Indian Ocean.
The steep green shores rise sharply from the blue water: the
earth, where trees have been felled to make roads, is reddish in
colour.

'Morning, sir.'

'Morning, Pilot. We'll dive in about twenty minutes' time.'

Just before six, when up top the first grey streaks of light are breaking through, the klaxon roars harshly, once, twice, the signal to dive. Men still half-asleep are flying out of their bunks before the Captain has taken his thumb off the push-button in the Conning Tower, and by the time he has clamped the hatch over his head and clambered down into the Control Room all hands are at their stations and the needle in the depth-gauge is swinging slowly past the 20-foot mark.

'Thirty feet,' orders the Captain.

'Thirty feet,' says Number One, both as acknowledgement of the order and as an order to the two men who, sitting in front of him on the port side of the Control Room, operate the controls of the hydroplanes.

Hydroplanes are horizontal rudders, one set forward and one set aft, which are tilted to alter the submarine's depth or to keep her steady at the depth ordered. Each man works his own control wheel, his eyes on the depth-gauge, and the bubble in the spirit-level.

The fore planesman, Bird the Second Cox'n, swings his wheel to the midships position, and mutters, 'Thirty feet, sir.'

At the order 'Watch Diving' the men disperse, leaving the men of the watch on duty to keep the ship at periscope depth on a north-easterly course, speed four knots towards the patrol area off Rangoon. Time for some sleep before breakfast.

'Whose watch?' asks the Captain.

'Mine, sir.' The sub can't deny it.

'It'll be light inside half-an-hour, Sub. Keep a good lookout, and if you think we're going too near the island, call me. In fact, call me when it's light enough to get a fix.'

'Aye aye, sir. Up periscope.'

'After planes relieved, sir. Thirty feet.'

'Very good.'

'Fore planes relieved, sir. Thirty feet.'

'Very good.'

'Helmsman relieved, sir, course oh-six-oh, telegraphs half ahead together.'

'Very good.'

The watch settles down, and nobody else is left in the Control Room. As the crew go for'ard to their quarters, the submarine's trim is upset; she becomes lighter in the stern, heavier in the bow. The Officer of the Watch adjusts this, indicating on an electric transmitter to men on watch elsewhere in the boat that they must flood water into the stern and amidships tanks, and pump water out forward. When the planesmen can keep their planes level, with the bubble in the centre of the spirit-level and the needle of the depth-gauge at the right depth, then the boat is more or less in trim. Flick off the indicator lights, move across to the periscope-well and jerk your hands upwards: the periscope, controlled from a lever operated by the Engine Room Artificer of the watch, slides up. Grab the handles, pull them down, watch for the dawn, the island and the enemy.

The day passed, like ninety per cent of all days on patrol, without incident. Watch relieved watch, meal followed meal, and only once was the Captain interrupted. This was during Number One's watch, in the forenoon, when he spotted an aircraft, a Jap seaplane flying south.

'Enemy aircraft, Red four five, sir, moving left to right.'

They kept an eye on it, through the small periscope, until it was lost to sight on the starboard bow. There were two periscopes, the big one for normal use, and a small one, not much thicker than a cigar at the top end, which had no magnification but made less track in the water and was less easily seen. It was used mainly during torpedo attacks, when the submarine was close to the target or to its escorts.

The Captain went back to his bunk.

He was worrying, though none of his officers would have known it. He was thinking about Japanese soldiers: if they met some, in Landing Craft, and they surrendered, what the hell could he do with them? There might be fifty, or a hundred, or more, and it wouldn't be possible to take more than ten into the submarine. Even five would be more than enough. Five, in fact, would be the limit. That might leave, say, a hundred and ninety-five men with their hands up. It was a tricky problem, and his future career could depend on it. It might be no use saying, 'I could only take five.' Someone might say, in Whitehall, 'A hundred and ninety-five men is a mass killing and that sort of thing just isn't done.' On the other hand, he'd be court-martialled if he left a Landing Craft afloat.

He'd take five, and the rest could drown. But they wouldn't drown, of course: the barracuda would see to that. You could always leave it to the fish, in these waters.

In the forward compartment, where the seamen lived, Wilkins lay in his hammock, wide awake. Sleep didn't come. All that came was a sort of cinema show, over and over again. He and his wife were in the first reel, on his last leave. It wasn't much of a leave, only a long week-end, three days, three nights in London. On the morning after his third night he had woken early when the alarm-clock rang, groped for it and pressed the button that stopped the noise. She hadn't woken, only smiled her cat's smile and murmured 'darling' in her sleep. He kissed her and still she slept, wearing the same soft smile, so he slid out of bed and shaved and dressed, then put the kettle on and brought two cups of tea on the tin tray and woke her up in a special way that she liked.

He left her crying in the bed, and he caught his train with her tear-wet face in his mind. Nobody, as far back as he could remember, had ever cried for him like that.

Then the letters were fewer, became formal and had no warmth. And the gossip in the other letters came instead.

In the last reel he saw her with the Pole, a lithe, amorous swine with plenty of money and a nice soft job in London. The words 'The End' flashed on the screen and he thought, 'This is where I came in.'

'Call the Red watch,' came the order, and Wilkins slid out of his hammock, quite ready to go on watch because he hadn't even taken his shoes off since the last one.

'Well,' observed Chief, 'if the Japs have evacuated Rangoon I reckon they've done it in rickshas. Five bloody days, and not a thing ... unless you people have had your eyes shut, of course.'

'When a man's just opened his eyes for the first time in five days, he's got a hell of a nerve to start making insinuations about other people's watch-keeping.'

'It does begin to look like no evacuation,' admitted the Captain.

'A blasted flop,' agreed Number One. 'This whole war's a bit of a flop, really. Nothing worth sinking anywhere.'

The submarine was on the surface, charging her batteries and making a slow progress up and down the ever-empty patrol area.

The Captain yawned. 'Well,' he murmured, 'perhaps, one day, we'll be allowed further down the Straits. Should be some pickings, at the bottom end.'

'What about the mines? Do we just pretend they aren't there?'

'They'll have to be passed, one day, won't they? The war can't end here.' Chief looked up quickly.

'They can give some other sucker that job. I prefer to go on breathing as long as possible.'

The Navigator appeared from the direction of the Control Room, his bare feet flip-flopping on the deck. 'Cipher coming through, sir,' he announced.

'Get your books ready, Chief.'

'Oh, Christ!' Chief heaved himself into a sitting position and fished about at the end of his bunk for the cipher books.

'I'll give you a hand,' volunteered the Navigator.

'Frightfully generous of you, old boy.' The signal was brought in, and they began to unravel the code.

'Good show!' exclaimed the Navigator, brightening up.

'What is it?'

'So far we've got, "Proceed – establish patrol —" '

'Come on, Chief – where?'

It turned out to be an area off the north-western tip of Sumatra.

'Doesn't sound very exciting.'

'Who the hell wants excitement?' asked Chief. 'Anyway, it can't be worse than this bloody place, can it?'

There was more to be deciphered, and this was more like it. A convoy of a dozen junks had left Singapore the day before, and Intelligence reported that they were heading up the outside of the island of Sumatra. *Seahound*'s orders were to intercept. The convoy was reported to have an escort of two anti-submarine launches.

'Come on, Pilot!' snapped the Captain. 'What course?'

He was thinking: 'About five hundred miles. To get there in time I must stay on the surface all the way. It's a risk, but I'll have to take it.'

'Chief.'

'Yes, sir?'

'Maximum revs, Chief, for thirty-six hours – will your engines stand it?'

'Doubt it, sir.'

'Well, they'll bloody well have to, anyway!' He pressed the buzzer for the Control Room messenger.

'Sir?'

'Tell the Officer of the Watch to come round to 200 degrees.'

'Two hundred degrees, sir. Aye aye, sir.' The Sub-Lieutenant answered the voice-pipe.

'Bridge.'

'From the Captain, sir, come round to two-double-oh.'

'Very good. Starboard fifteen.'

'Starboard fifteen, sir. Fifteen of starboard wheel on, sir.'

'Steer two-double-oh.'

'Steer two-double-oh, sir.'

'Bridge!'

'Bridge.'

'Course two-double-oh, sir.'

'Very good. Tell the Captain.'

Presently the Captain came on the bridge. 'Four hundred revs, Sub. The charge is broken.'

'Aye aye, sir. Control Room!'

'Control Room.'

'Four hundred revolutions.'

'Four hundred revolutions, sir. Four hundred revolutions on, sir.'

The Navigator shouted up that the course should be two-oh-three degrees, and they steered the new course.

'Where are we going, sir?'

'Somewhere off Sabang. Junk convoy coming up, escorted.'

'Escorted, sir?'

'That's what I said. Four-two-oh revs.'

'Four-two-oh revs, sir.'

In the Engine Room, Chief was biting his finger-nails. He was sure his engines would fall to bits before they got there.

'God damn it!' he muttered, as he passed through the Control Room on his way back to the Wardroom.

E.R.A. Featherstone looked at him sympathetically.

'They're always the bloody same, sir. Full speed, and flip the bloody engines. I dunno.'

'Come here, Sub.'

The Captain had been sitting deep in thought at the Wardroom table, drawing things occasionally on a piece of signal pad. Sub took a seat beside him and waited.

'Convoy of junks. Two escorts. The escorts probably have nothing bigger than some sort of pom-poms. Probably some point fives. We'll surface on the bow of the convoy, stern towards them and draw the escorts off. Engage one over our quarter with the three-inch, keeping the range steady, and use the Oerlikon on the other if it's in range. Both the escorts'll have to be knocked off before we go for the junks, and we'll take them afterwards by boarding, as usual. You'll have to be bloody quick, and I'll take you from one to the other as fast as I can.'

'There'll be a lot of Chinese crew to look after, sir.'

'Yes – we'll leave the smallest junk to the last, and leave all the crews in her. You won't have to board that one. All clear?'

'Yes, sir. I'll brief the Gunlayer and Wilkins.'

'May I be permitted to ask a question?' asked Chief, in a sarcastic tone of voice.

They looked at him. 'Well?'

'Why don't we surface bows on to the target?'

'Because, you bloody fool, our only advantage is the range of the three-inch. If we attack bows on, we get closer, and at close range they can give us hell. Not only that: when we get to a certain point we have to turn away, and that gives them a nice big target.'

Chief had no comment.

*

63

The Sub pulled a tin of Players out of his drawer, extracted a cigarette. He waved the tin towards Tommy, the Navigator.

'Smoke?'

'No, thanks.' The Navigator was sitting in a corner of the Wardroom, fiddling with a piece of string. He often sat like that, doing nothing, a dreamy look on his face. He's a nice fellow, thought the Sub, and a good navigator: but he's so damn quiet that sometimes he gives me the creeps. Anyone could see that the man was too old for his job: he should have been a First Lieutenant at least, by now.

'Tommy: why don't you ever talk about the time you were sunk, about the escape?'

'There's nothing to tell.' The Navigator spoke quickly, not looking at the Sub. 'We were sunk, that's all: I got out with eight men.'

The submarine was on the surface, racing southwards through the night. The Captain and Number One were on the bridge: Chief was nursing his engines. Sub and the Navigator sat alone in the Wardroom.

'H'm. I wish you'd tell me all about it. I often wonder what it'd be like in real earnest: it's easy enough in the tank at Block-house, of course, but I always wonder if it's so damn simple when you have to do it from a submarine.'

'There's nothing to worry about: it's just a matter of keeping your head and carrying out the drill, that's all. It's easy when you come to do it.'

Again the Navigator spoke fast, tonelessly, as though he was repeating a formula.

'There's nothing to worry about.' As he spoke, his mind went back as it did so often, always in the nightmare when he slept and now sometimes as a daydream, too. In every detail he re-lived the sinking and the escape ... three years ago, yet it might have happened yesterday.

In the for'ard compartment, between the reload torpedoes in their racks, he watched the angle increase as the submarine shot towards the bottom. The crash of the collision still rang deafen-ingly in his ears, he clung to one of the curved bars that held the torpedoes in their racks, and he thought to himself, This is it, it's happened. Now I'll know the answer. He was shut off in the

64

compartment, a water-tight door clamped between it and the rest of the submarine. He had with him a Petty Officer Higham, and seven seamen. They were on their way to the bottom, stern first, the after part of the submarine flooded and dragging them down. His men stood clinging to the sides, their eyes on his face, hopeless eyes in everything except their one, slight hope: himself.

It hadn't been difficult, being a submariner, except for the doubt that came occasionally: If *this* happened, could I see it through? Would I keep my head, justify my training and my existence as an officer? Well, it had come, here it was, and the thud was soft, dull, as the stern of the submarine bit into the mud. The submarine quivered, staggered, and the men's eyes searched the bulkheads expecting to see the plates open, cracks appear, expecting the rush of pressure and the quick but not necessarily pleasant end. Slowly the angle lessened as the submarine's bow sank: she steadied with an angle of only five degrees fore-and-aft.

Tommy heard his voice say, 'Take it easy. There's plenty of time now to get out. We're not in very deep water.'

' 'Ow deep is it, sir?' asked Payne, the leading torpedoman. He might have been asking the question on the surface, wanting to know how much cable they'd have to let out when they anchored for a night between exercises.

'Only a few fathoms.' He was the Torpedo Officer, not the Navigator, in this submarine: he hadn't much idea of the depth of water.

He moved along to the after bulkhead, turned the valve-wheel on the small diameter tube that connected with the next compartment. As the valve opened, a stream of water flew like a bullet past his face. He shut the valve: they could all see what that meant: they were the only ones left.

Bertram, a young torpedo-man, muttered, 'P'raps they're better off 'n what we are.' The Petty Officer rounded on him quickly.

'Shut y' mouth, y' damn fool. No air to waste 'ere.' He looked at Tommy. 'Shall I try the salvage blow, sir?'

'No. Waste of time.' They'd all heard and felt the collision: aft of this bulkhead, the whole side of the submarine must have been split open. The men stood looking at him, waiting for orders.

The hatch over his head, at the after end of the compartment, was not an escape hatch but the ordinary one used for coming and going when the submarine was in harbour. For a moment he thought: If I told myself this was a dream, unreal, if I climbed up the ladder and threw open the hatch, should I not find myself in the bright, chill air, hear the engines in the other submarines charging their batteries alongside, find Number One standing on the casing, shouting, 'Come on! Get a move on! Are those torpedoes going to take all next week to load?'

No, perhaps not. It looked real enough, on the men's faces. He grinned at Higham.

'Well, looks like we'll have to get our feet wet. Gather round me here, all of you. Just in case you need reminding, I'll run through the drill for escaping ... you've all done it in the tank at Blockhouse: well, it'll be exactly the same now. Keep your heads, don't hurry, take it easy, stick to the drill, and we'll be up in the fresh air in next to no time.'

He began to talk about the escape apparatus, how easy, how foolproof it was: while he spoke, he thought how easy it would be for everything to go wrong.

The principle was simple enough. Around the escape hatch, strung up to the deckhead, was a thing called a Twill Trunk. It was a cylinder, made of twill, that could be let down to form a tube from the hatch down into the compartment: lines attached to its bottom edge could be secured to fittings in the compartment to hold the trunk rigidly and vertically in place. A steel ladder fitted up to the hatch inside the trunk.

Inside the compartment the pressure was atmospheric: outside, sea-pressure, forcing down on the hull, held the hatches shut.

There was a flood valve in the compartment, a big brass wheel that you could turn to let the sea in. This was the procedure: open the flood-valve, the water rises until it can rise no more because it is met by an equal pressure from the air which it has compressed at the top of the compartment. The water covers the lower part of the twill trunk. Then one man goes under the water, up inside the trunk, and opens the vent in the escape

66

hatch. Air rushes out and the water rises inside the trunk, right up to the hatch. The pressure is then equal on either side of the hatch: open it, climb down the ladder and rejoin the men in the compartment: send them out, one by one, to float up to the surface, breathing freely from the oxygen sets which they wear strapped on their chests.

'How many sets have we got, Higham?'

'One each and some to spare, sir.'

'Pass me one over.'

The emergency lanterns glowed faintly, throwing grotesque shadows on the curved steel walls of their prison. The compartment had for months been the home of these men: their bedroom, dining-room, sitting-room. Here they sat and wrote their letters home, drank their tots of rum and swung comfortably asleep in their hammocks. Now they were preparing to fill it with water, flood it, open it up, leave it to the fishes. Anyway, at all costs, leave it.

He put the set on, adjusted the straps, began to explain and demonstrate its use, the different valves, how to hold the mouthpiece, how to puncture the oxygen flask.

'See? It's dead easy. The only thing is, keep your heads, don't get excited. Flooding makes a hell of a row: remember it, at Blockhouse? At first you may find difficulty in breathing from your set: if you do, don't tear it off: raise your hand like this, and I or Higham'll fix it for you. Payne, you know all about it, don't you?'

Payne said that he did indeed know only too much about the flippin' sets. He'd rather not use one, rather go up in a free ascent, holding his breath.

'You'll wear a set, Payne.'

'Aye aye, sir.'

Well, he'd explained it all: better get a move on now. Tommy said to Higham, 'Rig the twill trunk.' While Higham and Payne worked at it, Tommy told the others to start getting their sets on: he moved round, helping them to adjust the straps. Soon they were ready, the trunking lashed firmly in place, the men standing by with the yellow sets on their chests. God, how lonely it was.

'Crack the valve.' To move the wheel that first inch took

nearly ten minutes. Only very slightly open, the noise of the water forcing in was already deafening. Tommy signalled to Higham to open the flood-valve to its full extent, and the roar hit them, struck them, left them gasping as the water rose to lap over their feet: their ears began to deaden under the rising pressure. Eyes were on him, several pairs of eyes swimming in the sound, all staring at him. It was up to him to show that everything was all right, everything under control: he grinned, his face deliberately in the light of one of the lanterns: nonchalantly he studied his watch without noticing the time. The water was up around his knees: he looked across at the base of the twill trunk, thought, It won't be long now. He looked around the compartment where the men stood motionless: each wore his oxygen set, the bag blown up with oxygen from the manifold in the corner of the compartment. Later, when he was ready and the hatch was open, he'd tell them to start breathing from their sets: then they'd put the mouthpieces in their mouths, blow all the air out of their lungs through their noses, put on the nose-clips, open the valves below the mouthpieces and start breathing oxygen. That would be later: he'd have to do it himself, first, before he ducked under the water and climbed up into the trunk to get the hatch open. They'd be able to see how he did it, before they did it themselves.

The water was rising less fast, the noise was less. The pressure was an iron clamp around his head. He looked at the trunk and saw that its base was well covered. The water rose to chest-level: Timmins, a torpedoman whose height was not much over five feet, was standing on a box, where Higham had placed him.

A little boy saying, 'Look, Uncle, I'm as big as you!' Little boys with marbles, air-guns and catapults, bees humming in the lavender, trees moving gently in the soft breeze of an English summer's day. The week-end dance, the pint of beer in the local, the old Baby Austin that you bought for a fiver. The only way to get back to any of it was through that blasted trunk. Some of these men had wives and children.

The water had stopped, only a soft hissing came from the corner where the flood-valve was. Tommy felt giddy from the crippling pressure. He wondered if the men would stand up to it much longer as he said, 'Right, now I'm leaving you for a few minutes, to get that hatch open. Higham, take charge while I'm away. If I'm not back in fifteen minutes, send Payne up to see what's wrong.'

'Aye aye, sir.'

They watched him closely as he went through the routine with his set. Just as he was about to duck under water, under the edge of the trunk, he remembered that he might need a wheel-spanner for the vent in the hatch. There was one hanging from an air-pipe behind Payne: Tommy pointed at it, held out his hand, and Payne quickly passed it across.

He didn't want to duck down and miss the trunking, come up into the light again in the circle of anxious faces: he stood right against the side of the trunk, grasped the bottom edge before he ducked. He wondered whether or not he should open the exhaust valve on his oxygen bag: what had the instructors said, at Blockhouse? He couldn't remember; he decided to leave it shut. After all, he'd be in the air again when he came up inside the trunking, until he got the valve open in the hatch. That would be the time to open the exhaust, shut it again when he returned to the compartment.

He ducked into the dark water, holding the edge of the trunk: forced himself down hard, edged forward until he felt the edge of the trunking pass over his head. Then he stood up inside the trunk, his hands on the ladder: he climbed up, his head in air not water, but still breathing oxygen. He held the side of the ladder with his right hand: his left, holding the wheel-spanner, he held up over his head to feel for the hatch. He hadn't counted the rungs as he climbed, and now he thought, I must be nearly at the top. His hand found no ceiling in the dark, though, and he climbed another rung. His goggles had already leaked, salt water stung his eyes. Still that hatch was not in reach: he took another upward step, and the wheel-spanner clanged loudly on the inside of the hatch. He braced himself with both feet on the same rung, his back supported against the upper part of the twill trunk, and he transferred the wheel-spanner to his right hand. With his left he found the little T-bar on the vent, and he fitted the knuckles of the spanner across it, pressed anti-clockwise: his hands were almost numb from the cold water. The vent didn't move; he rested, began again, and his stiff fingers slipped, dropped the spanner.

He heard it clang off a rung of the ladder, somewhere in front of his face, and he heard another clang as it hit the deck. He began slowly climbing down, feeling for the rungs below him at each step. He thought to himself, Take it easy, now: there's no hurry. As he went down into the water, pulling himself down into the icy blackness right down on to his knees at the bottom of the ladder, he felt the pressure in his breathing-set increase until it stopped him breathing out. He breathed in, easily, but he couldn't force his breath back into the bag. For a moment panic flared in his mind, then he remembered, opened the exhaust valve: the pressure fell away at once and he could breathe again. He began to grope around on the deck.

It wasn't there. He thought, I can't go back into the compartment without having the job done. Still he couldn't find the wheel-spanner: he started a new, systematic search, covering the deck area under the trunk methodically, strip by strip. He could only use one hand, because he needed the other for holding himself down. The wheel-spanner was not there. He paused, and his brain gave him the clue: it shouldn't have clanged, not if it hit the deck! He ran his free hand over the lower rungs of the ladder; almost immediately he found it, hanging from the second rung by its hook. Slowly he began to climb back to the hatch, congratulated himself when he remembered to shut the exhaust valve before he came out of the water.

This time he went one rung higher on the ladder: stooped as he was, it gave him a better purchase on the spanner. He pressed hard, and felt the vent begin to open. A minute later the water was rising, a tearing sound in his ears as the trapped air rushed out through the tiny aperture. When he knew that the trunking was flooded, he began numbly to work at the hatch. The pressure fought his breath again, and once more he opened the vent at the bottom corner of the bag, once more felt the relief of being able to breathe comfortably. His arms felt heavy, pain working up from the wrists: he could only just feel with his frozen fingers. He wondered how long he'd been working, whether they'd be getting worried in the compartment: he could imagine Payne preparing to come up and drag his body out of the way of the hatch.

The hatch was free; he braced himself on the ladder, got his shoulders under the hatch, head bent forward, and he forced himself upwards. The hatch rose: he shifted, got the palms of his hands under it, pushed hard: it clanged back and over his head there was grey light filtering down from the surface, the black streak of the jumping-wire a quivering line across it. He thought, I must remember to warn them about that: when men let themselves go fast, straight from the hatch, they could hit the wire and either knock themselves out or have their sets torn off. He began to climb slowly down the ladder, rung by rung: felt the bottom of the trunking, eased himself under it: and rose to his feet in the dimly illuminated compartment.

They looked as much surprised as relieved to see him back. When he had shut the valves and pulled the mouthpiece out of his mouth, he said, 'Everything's fine. The hatch is open, and we can't be very deep. It's quite light, when you look up. Remember to watch out for the jumping-wire: get on to the side of the casing before you let go, and use the apron on your sets to slow yourselves down.'

He spoke in jerks, panting from the exertion. Looking at his fingers, he was surprised to see that they still belonged to him, connected with bones and flesh: he couldn't feel them. There was no skin on his knuckles, the flesh showed pink and bloodless.

'Right, Higham: you first. I'll point at each of you in turn after that, at two-minute intervals. Payne, you'll be last, except for me. All right?'

They all nodded. He was keeping Payne to the last as a useful hand in case one of the others bungled it, got himself stuck.

'Start breathing from your sets.' He watched them as they began to go through the drill. Then, a minute later, he nodded at Higham, pointed at the trunking. Higham vanished under the edge of the trunking. Every two minutes, Tommy sent another man after him: he checked the timing carefully, by counting.

Last of all he nodded across at Payne. Payne grinned, held out his right hand: cursing the waste of time and the film-like gesture, Tommy shook hands with him. Then he withdrew his hand, pointed at the trunking. Payne nodded, lowered himself into the water.

Tommy, alone in the compartment, made himself wait twice the interval of two minutes before he started. While he waited, there was no sense of success in his mind: outside the hatch, in the hatch, there could be a solid block of tangled bodies.

For the second time, he lowered himself into the still black water: the lantern still shone quietly in the false and temporary breathing-space. He found the ladder, climbed: with an effort he made himself look up. The hatch was clear: he held the rungs with his hands curved under them, holding himself down from the upward rush that could kill him in the hatch.

Grasping the edges, he rose through the hatch, stopped in the gap in the casing while he opened the valve on his oxygen bottle: the breath came more easily, and he wondered why at this, of all times, the goggles were keeping the water out of his eyes. He had never been through the practice tank without them leaking. He knelt on the casing, his fingers straining to keep him down, locked in the holes, and he edged to the side so that when he let himself go he'd miss the wire that stretched over his head. At other times, he had leant on that wire while he chatted in the sunlight.

One hand still holding on, he used the other to free the rubber apron which would act as a sort of parachute in reverse: held out in both hands it would resist the water, slow his ascent to the surface.

He let go, and at once floated clear of the casing: he arched his body, head back and chest out, his hands extending the apron. The jumping-wire flashed past him as he rose: his ears were blowing out of his head, the veins in his head were expanding, bursting as the pressure lessened: he was rising too fast and there was nothing he could do about it. The light grew, burst in his face as a wave hit him, rolled him over: his brain exploded in a million fragmented moments of the past two hours, and when the men in the rescue craft pulled him out of the water they thought that he was dead....

Tommy looked up from where he sat slumped over the ward-room table. Sub had turned in. Tommy wondered if people noticed when he went through his daydream business. He thought, I went through that once, and you'd think that once was enough: now I go through it every ten days.

There wasn't much justice in it. There was only one consolation: having done that, having passed the highest test of submarining, he wanted nothing more. To him, there was no higher peak. He had lived his day, fought his war and won it. Now, all that he wanted was a quiet billet. He'd be on watch, in half an hour.

'Up periscope,' ordered the Sub. At the lift of the lever, the periscope rose quickly, hissing as the wires ran round the sheaves on the deckhead.

'Stand by for a fix.' The messenger grabbed a signal-pad and poised a pencil over it.

Sub took three bearings, and laid the position off on the chart. They were patrolling off the island, up and down an East–West line for three miles in each direction. It was the second day in the area, and so far they had seen nothing, except for seagulls that glided down on the wind and circled the periscope.

Four o'clock came, and Number One took over the watch. Sub sat down to tea, buttered a piece of bread an inch thick and covered it with sardines. He had it half-way to his mouth when Number One's voice came, sharp and urgent.

'Captain, sir!'

The Captain spilled his tea, and rushed into the Control Room. Sub lowered his sardines, and he and the Navigator looked at each other, wondering, hoping.

'Diving stations!'

The men were in their places, all eyes on the Captain, who hung on to the periscope, absorbed, silent. He moved it round, a little this way and that.

Number One was intent on his own job, watching the depth and the trim.

'Steer one-five-oh,' ordered the Captain. He swept round, all the horizon and the sky, then stopped again on the target, whatever it was. Suddenly he jerked the handles of the periscope up and stepped back, rubbing his chin, thoughtfully. As he stepped back, Featherstone pressed down the lever that sent the periscope back into its well.

The Captain looked round.

'It's the convoy,' he said. 'About a dozen junks. Can't see any escort yet.' The low hum of the motors and the ticking of the electric log were the only sounds in the Control Room.

Two minutes passed. 'Up periscope.'

'There they are. Two of them. Stand by Gun Action. Down periscope.'

The routine swung into action, quickly and quietly.

'Gun's crew closed up, sir.'

'Very good. Up periscope.' For a moment he searched the horizon all round. Then, back on the target, he said:

'Target an M/L. Range five thousand yards. Bearing will be about green one-five-oh. Shoot.'

'Deflection, sir?'

'Set no deflection.' Sub passed the orders to the Gun's crew. The Captain spoke again: 'Wilkins.'

'Sir?'

'Your target is the other M/L. She'll be right astern. You take the one to the right, understand?'

'Aye aye, sir.'

'Starboard twenty, group up, fifty feet.'

The submarine began to turn on to her attacking course, nosing down to fifty feet and increasing speed.

'Steer three-one-five,' ordered the Captain.

Wilkins' eyes were hard and bright, his mouth a thin line. Jimmy was wishing he wasn't a First Lieutenant, tied down to a job in the Control Room and only hearing the noise of the action. Tommy was checking the depth of the water, on the chart.

Chief was thinking that this was one of the times when he'd rather be an executive officer than an engineer. To be down below, working blindly while the men on the gun and the bridge fought a battle, gave little satisfaction. He looked at the Sub, whose face showed only eagerness, impatience, and he thought, 'Damned if I can understand that kid! He doesn't know what the hell's going to happen up there, he hasn't even seen it. He's like a terrier: get at it, boy, seek him out!'

In most faces, looking round the Control Room, Chief saw tension, anxiety. Only the duller ones showed little feeling, and Sub was not by any means dull or insensitive. Chief thought that if this was an American film, Sub's apparently fearless belligerence would be explained by his old mother having been raped by a Japanese soldier in Hong Hong. Chief knew of no such reason for the boy's fanaticism.

If the Sub had known that Chief regarded him as a fanatic, he would have laughed: not now, but later, he would have laughed. Now, his palms were running with sweat, his heart was pounding and in his mind he was saying a prayer: God, don't let me lose my head. Don't let them know that the last few minutes before we surface for a gun action are minutes of torture. He thought, If they saw how scared I was, they'd think that it was my skin that I was scared for, they'd think I was frightened of being killed. They wouldn't believe that I was terrified of only one thing, of making a fool of myself, of messing up the shoot, letting down the Gun's Crew, proving myself useless.

At Dartmouth, he had been of little use, because he had disliked the life, the routine, the stiffness: now, at sea, he was proving to himself that he was not useless, that he could do anything as well as anyone else, that the Cadet at Dartmouth had not been John Ferris, but a John Ferris under the influence of Dartmouth.

'Oh, Christ!' he thought, 'Let's get up there, get on with it!' After the first shot had been fired, the relief was always tremendous: between shouting directions to the Gun's Crew and observing the fall of shot, he would wonder to himself what on earth he had been worrying about. This was easy: it always was.

'Course three-one-five, sir,' reported the helmsman.

'Fifty feet, sir,' growled the Second Cox'n.

'Full ahead together.' The Captain had one foot on the bottom of the ladder. 'Surface!'

Number One had a whistle between his teeth. When the needle in the depth-gauge passed the fifteen-foot mark, he blew it, and the hatches were flung open as the boat surfaced.

Blinding sunshine met them harshly after the soft artificial

75

light in the submarine. There was the convoy, a straggle of nine or ten junks of varying sizes, just about right astern. Ahead of the convoy, broadside on to the submarine's stern, was one of the anti-submarine launches. She was much the same size and shape as the usual British type of motor launch, the bridge high for her length, quick-firing guns dotted about her bridge and stern.

Away from the island, between the convoy and the submarine and keeping abreast of the centre of the convoy, was a second craft of the same class.

It took an effort to absorb this picture, so suddenly in view and so different from the picture that had been forming in their minds while they were waiting under water, but habit and the clear-cut orders overrode the momentary strangeness.

The three-inch fired, and the enemy launch that had been ahead of the convoy swung away.

'They're running away, by God!' muttered the Captain.

'Right eight, up four hundred, shoot!'

But the launch was not running away: that swerve was only panic, or an error by the helmsman. Now she was swinging back again, heading straight for the submarine.

'Down two hundred, shoot!'

The other launch was also coming towards them, from the port quarter. Wilkins tried his Oerlikon for range, but the only splashes he could see were a long way short. He waited, watching his target.

The third shot fell close to the first launch.

'Down one hundred, shoot!' A few moments passed before they saw the shell explode in the launch's bridge. A second hit, and the enemy was on fire. One more, and they could leave her where she was for the time being and pay a little attention to the other one.

The Captain put his mouth to the mouth-pipe.

'Slow ahead together!' he bellowed. He was going to let the second escort close in while the gun was trained round to the new target.

Come into my parlour, said the spider to the fly, and I'll blast you over my port quarter.

'Steer two-nine-oh.'

The fourth shot was a hit, so was the sixth and the seventh and eighth, and that was enough, more than enough for the second enemy, who lay stopped and sinking.

It was odd, this voice business: when he had been shouting at the Gun's Crew, over the combined noise of the diesels, the Captain's orders, the gun's firing and the roar of the Oerlikon as Wilkins tried the range, Sub found that he couldn't hear his own voice any more. After a few actions, though, when he found that the men on the gun had heard every word, he realized that it was his own ears and not his voice that was to blame.

'She's going, sir!' As he spoke, the second launch slowly disappeared. There were no survivors that anyone could see.

'Starboard twenty, half ahead together. Stand by, Boarding Party.' The Captain straightened up from the voice-pipe, and shouted up at the Sub as he sat on the front edge of the bridge, 'We'll see if there are any survivors in that wreck, before we round up the junks.' He pointed at the first launch, now low in the water, stopped and smouldering.

It had been ridiculously easy, thanks to a well-trained Gun's Crew. It was often like that: when you expected something to be rough, it came smooth and simple, and when you came up for an easy little shoot some damn thing like an aeroplane turned up and queered the pitch.

The launch had sunk several feet lower in the water. The shattered bridge had bodies and parts of bodies strewn about it. One dead sailor, evidently killed at his gun, lay slumped grotesquely across it.

'Slow together,' ordered the Captain into the voice-pipe. 'Put one shot into his water-line as we pass, Sub.'

Sub shouted to the Gun's Crew: 'No deflection, no range – one shot into the water-line amidships, as we pass.'

'Aye aye, sir,' sang out the Gunlayer, and the Loader shoved a shell into the breech. The Gun's Crew were black with cordite smoke, the whites of their eyes bright in their dark faces. The Gunlayer bent to his telescope, his hand on the trigger, and it was as the submarine drew level, about thirty yards away from the wreck, that it happened. The twisted figure in the sinking craft straightened itself on the gun, which was something like an Oerlikon, and a stream of explosive bullets lashed across the gap. The wounded man's aim was bad, and the burst flew high. On *Seahound*'s bridge the Vickers machine-gunner brought his sights on and pulled the trigger, but nothing happened. His gun was jammed. In a last effort the Jap forced up on the shoulder-rests of his gun, and at the moment that the three-inch shell burst and blew out the side of the enemy launch, Able Seaman Wilkins was cut almost in half.

Now for the junks, scattered, except for a nucleus of five that hung together like frightened sheep seeking comfort in numbers, and these could safely be left to wait until the odd ones had been rounded up.

One had been sunk, and in one the charge had just exploded so that she had begun to settle in the water, when the unexpected happened again. Sub and his five men were in number three, one of the biggest. Except for Bird, they were all down below. The submarine lay alongside, seven Chinese from the first two junks squatting on the casing, guarded by the Gun-layer who had a revolver in one of his enormous fists.

Suddenly the Captain shouted from the submarine's bridge: 'Get those men into the junk – I'm going to dive!'

The Gunlayer rushed his Chinese forward and over the side, waving his gun and shouting abuse which they could hardly be expected to understand in detail but which was plain enough in effect.

'Gar, you shower of flippin' sods! Get on, you flippin' fowls, I'll make you jump!'

Bird, on the junk's deck, raised his eyebrows and murmured a protest as he cast off the line and the Gunlayer leaped across the gap, just in time. The submarine backed away, full speed astern on the motors; the bridge was empty and the vents crashed open, the air roared out and she dived stern first.

Sub was on deck in time to see the bridge disappear, and looking around for a reason for this remarkable manoeuvre he saw it at once. An aircraft was approaching at a height of about two thousand feet from the direction of Sumatra.

'Put the extra Chinks down below, Bird. Boarding Party go below, all of you. Keep an eye on the Chinks and if any of them make any trouble, kill them.'

'Aye aye, sir.' The Boarding Party vanished.

The junks' crew, three men, sat around on deck looking quite normal except at close quarters, when their expressions were those of rabbits with a snake in their hutch. Sub was crouching under the poop, his ·38 revolver well in view, aimed at the senior member.

The aircraft lost height, and circled slowly. To save time, Sub indicated to the crew that they were to sail towards the nearest junk.

The airman could see nothing unusual. The escorts had been sunk: the submarine had dived, and presumably he had frightened it away. There was nothing he could do! Banking sharply, he straightened his course and headed away to report back to his base in Sumatra.

'Bird!'

'Sir?'

'All clear. Leave two hands to watch the Wogs. You, Shadwell and Parrot come up here.'

The three men appeared out of the musty hatch. The Gunlayer followed them, looking hurt that he hadn't been mentioned. Sub pointed to the nearest junk, a hundred yards away.

'We'll take that one now. She's smaller and easier to handle, so we'll transfer to her and sink this one. Then we'll go around the fleet leaving our cards.'

The junk's crew were no seamen, and ran their junk alongside the other with a crash of straining timbers. The Chinese were sent over into the smaller craft, and after placing the charge Sub sent his men over. He fired the charge and followed them. They cast off, and headed for the bunch of five junks that still hung together, waiting their turn in a conveniently close formation.

Bird eased himself into a languid position in the bow of the junk, and remarked that it reminded him of his last season at Cowes.

'Simply spiffin' old boy, it was,' he told the Gunlayer.

'Silly bastard.'

Bird began to sing the Eton boating song.

Parrot came for'ard and looked down at Bird. 'Shut up,' he

said, quietly. Bird stopped singing, a look of surprise on his big face.

''Oo d'you think yer talking to, eh?'

'You came up through the Guntower hatch, didn't you, same as Guns 'ere?'

'I did – what of it?'

'You didn't see Wilky, did yer?'

'No – what d'yer mean?'

'I mean he's dead. I mean 'is guts are all over the flippin' bridge. That's what I mean.'

There was a bang from the junk which they had just left; rocking slightly, she began to sink.

CHAPTER FOUR

'Not a bad job you did, Sub.'

From the Captain, that was a startling recommend.

The submarine was dived again, waiting for dark.

Number One said, 'If any officer in Naval history has lost his first nine commands quite so fast, I'd be very surprised.'

The Captain was thinking that on paper, in the patrol report, it looked well enough. Two anti-submarine launches, nine junks, a couple of dozen Japanese sailors and a few officers. Against that, one British sailor. Yes, it looked like a battle won. But to Arthur Hallet's private mind he'd have given a year's seniority not to have met that convoy. In an operational submarine, discipline was real. It meant complete understanding between officer and man, the sacrifice of any personal feelings when they counted against efficiency, the discarding of any formality that counted against the general welfare. Nobody was just a name and a number. Every man was a complete individual, a separate, vital component of the fighting machine.

'Basher' Wilkins, as they called him in the seamen's mess, had been one of them, part of *Seahound* herself. Now what remained of him was on the bottom, heavily weighted, wrapped in a Union Jack. No man who had stood in the Control Room while the Captain read the simple prayers, no man who had been on the bridge when 'Basher' took his last, solitary dive, would ever forget this day, nor ever make peace with a Jap.

'Where do we go from here, sir?' Number One asked the question as the Captain turned back from the chart table. He brought the chart with him, spread it on the wardroom table.

Off the extreme north-western tip of Sumatra is an island called Sabang. Inside the island, through a narrow bottleneck entrance, is a wide enclosed bay. The Captain pointed his pencil at the mainland coast inside the bay.

'In there,' he said, 'are jetties with cranes on them, storage sheds and an oil tank. I think we'll nip in tomorrow and shake 'em up.'

Chief sat up quickly.

'But sir! How do we get out, afterwards?'

'Who's to stop us?'

'They may have a patrol-boat, or aircraft. May be shore batteries. Think of my wife!'

'Either we'll get out dived, or we'll stay in until dark and get out on the surface at night. And that's enough comment from you. Pilot!'

'Sir?'

'Lay off a course to pass close outside Sabang, to enter from the East.'

'Aye aye, sir.'

'Sub!'

'Sir?'

'Is the Gunlayer doing a routine on the gun tonight?'

'Yes, sir.'

'How much ammunition left?'

'Only used about twenty rounds, sir.'

'I asked how much was left, not how much you'd used.'

'I'll check up, sir.'

'You ought to bloody well know.'

Chief, who knew trouble when he smelt it, wandered quietly off to the Engine Room.

'Signal coming through, sir.'

When it was deciphered, it was not received with any warmth. It was an Air/Sea Rescue signal, a report of an American bomber shot down, an order to proceed to a certain position and look for the survivors who, it was hoped, were still alive in a rubber dinghy. These signals were not at all unusual, and as most of them resulted in fruitless search because of an incorrectly reported position, nobody ever got very excited.

'God damn and blast,' said the Captain. 'All right, Pilot, put it on the chart and let's see.'

It meant all night at full speed again, and Chief shut his eyes as though the thought hurt him more than it would his engines. He lay down and pretended to go to sleep: there was less likelihood of being asked to do anything.

'Say,' began the aviator whose aircraft had bought it over Bangkok. 'Say, do you guys know how to shoot crap?'

Chief opened one eye. The Americans were sitting round the wardroom table.

'No,' said the Chief, and closed the eye.

'Gen'lemen,' said the Yank, looking round at the men in their bunks, 'I guess we're gonna have to i-nitiate you into a fine old American custom. Shootin' crap.'

'If you refer to the game you seem to have been playing all night,' said the Chief, 'I may as well tell you that I have not the slightest intention of having anything to do with it.'

'Tell me now,' asked the American, a look of friendly interest in his face, 'do you have anything in partic'lar against us guys? Or would you be what I heard a guy described as, once, "ant-i-social"?'

Chief grunted, and tried to go on sleeping.

'No, listen, now – er, what do the guys call you – Chief? – Tell me, now, what do you really think of us Americans?'

'That's not an easy question. But I once heard an Indian answer it rather well. He said: America is the only country in history that has passed from a state of barbarism to a state of decadence without first going through a state of civilization. That answer your question?'

'Uh-huh. I guess so. Didja hear the story about the G.I. and the English Tommy in London, Chiefy?'

'Go on.'

'Wal, seems the Britisher says to the G.I., the trouble with you Yanks, he says, is that you're over-paid, over-sexed and over here.'

'Hear, hear,' murmured the Chief.

'So the G.I. says to the Limey: The trouble with you is you're under-paid, under-sexed and under Eisenhower. How's that, boy?'

Chief drew himself out to his full length.

'I am not,' he said, 'a boy.'

'Guess he must be a goil,' said the Lootenant.

They had found the dinghy straight off with no difficulty. A signal had been sent with the names of the four survivors, and in reply had come an order to rendezvous with a Catalina flying boat which would take the airmen home to their base in India.

For once, some lives had been saved and not lost or taken. It was quite a change.

When they left, the Yankees shook Chief warmly by the hand.

'S'long, Chiefy. If you get leave, one day, come up and see us. We'll show you around, be glad to.'

'Thanks very much,' replied Chief. 'It's been nice having you.'

Everyone stared at them in amazement.

Chief's jaws were moving rhythmically up and down. He was chewing gum, or at any rate pretending to.

Over the dead-flat water the early morning mist was thick, blue-grey; an eerie light as the submarine nosed her way at periscope depth into the gap between the island and the mainland. There was not much room to spare, and the Captain himself was keeping the periscope watch, the Navigator standing ready to put a position on the chart as soon as the mist cleared enough to see the edges of the island. The feeling in the submarine was more tense than usual: the last submarine that the flotilla had lost was believed to have been lost in this placid, peaceful-looking bay.

'Clearing a bit. Take down these bearings.'

The fix on the chart showed that they were through the bottleneck, in the eastern end of the land-locked bay.

'All right, Pilot. Take over the watch.'

At the far end of the bay, on the coast of Sumatra, was the little harbour that was to be their target later in the day.

'Show as little periscope as possible.'

'Aye aye, sir.' In the warm silence the submarine crept steadily in between the smiling hills.

*

A messenger stood in the Wardroom entrance.

'From the First Lieutenant, sir, would you please come into the Control Room.'

The Captain swallowed a last forkful of corned beef, and joined Number One.

'What's up?'

'There's a small steamer at anchor off the port, sir. Red six-oh: she's camouflaged, a bit hard to see against the background.'

The Captain peered through the periscope.

'Well, I'm damned! You're quite right, Number One.'

He thought for a moment, rubbing his chin in the characteristic manner that they'd all seen so often when he stood at the periscope during an attack.

'Right. I'll sink her with one fish, then surface and bombard. We'll finish lunch first. Go to Diving Stations at one-thirty, Number One, but watch that ship and let me know if she starts getting under way. For God's sake don't show too much periscope.'

'Aye aye, sir.'

'Sub – tell the T.I. I'll be firing one torpedo at about one-thirty-five. River-steamer at anchor. When we've sunk her I'm going to surface and bombard.'

'Aye aye, sir.' Sub went forward.

The T.I. goggled. 'I don't believe it, sir. Fire a torpedo? From *this* ship. I thought we'd forgotten we 'ad any.'

'When we've sunk her, we'll be surfacing for a bombardment.'

'Ah, that's the stuff, sir. Got to throw the old gun in, too.'

'Steady as you go!' snaps the Captain, stooping at the periscope.

'Steady sir,' answers the helmsman. 'Course-one-nine-one.'

'Which tube, Sub?'

'Number three, sir.'

'Stand by number three tube.'

The man with the telephone set sends the message forward to the T.I.

'Number three ready, sir.'

'Stand by – fire!'

There's a thud that jars through the whole submarine as the torpedo is shot out of the tube. The air-pressure rises sharply and you swallow to clear your ears.

The man with the headphones, Saunders, reports, 'Torpedo running, sir.'

'Very good.' The Captain watches steadily through the periscope. Everyone is waiting for the bang they want to hear. Sometimes torpedoes go wrong and run crooked, off their course. Sometimes they miss. Up forward, the T.I. is murmuring under his breath, 'Oh Gawd, let it 'it, don't let it miss, Gawd, not this one.'

It hits all right, a roaring, shattering explosion, and the Captain smiles.

'Right. Stand by Gun Action.'

You've seen it earlier, through the periscope, and so has the Gunlayer. You know the targets: first the big oil storage tank, then the buildings and cranes on the jetty. But the storage tank stands among trees, and there's no sign of where the shell falls. Make a correction, any correction, and try again.

'Down eight hundred, shoot!'

You're in line, on the edge of the trees. 'Up twelve hundred, shoot!'

A film of dust rises through the tall trees, just short of the tank. 'Up four hundred, shoot!'

A hit, a flash of orange flame on the target. No more corrections: rapid fire.

A gun is firing from the harbour area, and the shots are not far off. That's a job for Rogers, the newly-promoted Oerlikon gunner. He gives it a long burst, and the firing stops. Rogers quickly changes the magazine on his gun and waits, watching for any more opposition.

The oil tank is finished now, and looks strangely like the stem of a giant mushroom, the top of which is composed of flames and black, oily smoke.

The Oerlikon is firing again: more opposition from a shore battery, one of whose shots at this moment has scrunched overhead, a noise like tearing calico: the splash goes up a long way over on their starboard quarter. Rogers has changed the pan on his gun, but his continued fire has no apparent effect on the enemy.

'Stop that bugger, Sub!'

The Sub yells over the front of the bridge to the crew of the three-inch: 'Shift target left: gun battery behind the left edge of the harbour: under the white smoke-cloud.'

The Gunlayer raises his left hand, thumb uppermost, in acknowledgement as he shows the Trainer the target.

'Down eight hundred, shoot!' The first round at the Jap battery hurtles away as one more enemy shot rips across astern.

'Down two hundred, shoot!'

It looks like a near miss, that one.

'No correction, shoot!' and as the splash from the enemy's shell drenches the Gun's Crew, the Captain orders full speed ahead to upset the Jap's calculations.

'Nice work, Sub!' That last one hit the battery. Two more shots in the same place, and still no answering fire: it seems to have done the trick.

Shift target to the jetty, and a crane goes over on its side. Three or four men rush out of the sheds, make for the trees as shells begin to land in the wooden buildings.

In ten minutes the little port is wrecked. In front of the background of the blazing oil tank, four other fires are blazing and spreading. Two cranes are finished for good, and a barge, the only thing that was left afloat after you'd torpedoed the steamer, is sunk.

Cease fire, blow your whistle. Take a last look, before you dive. They'll remember this day, ashore.

You shout to the Gun's Crew: 'Good shooting!' and they grin, showing white teeth in their blackened, happy faces.

Rogers, the man who had taken Wilkins' place as Oerlikon gunner, sat in the Seamen's Mess, peeling potatoes.

'Lieutenant Commander 'Allet,' he announced, 'is the best flippin' C.O. I ever served with.'

'Ah,' agreed a hard-faced man they called Dodger. 'Reckon we've got a good lad, there.'

'If any bastard in this flippin' ship likes to argue with me,' continued Rogers, 'I'll ram 'is teeth dahn 'is flippin' throat.'

'You always was one for an argument,' commented Shadwell, from the depths of a hammock.

Rogers looked at him. 'I was up on the bridge just now, Shaddy, and when we was finished flippin' the place up, and there was more smoke and flames than that on the flippin' beach, I saw the old man lookin' at it, steady-like, like 'e was drinking it in. When 'e turned round to pass some flippin' remark to Subby, 'e saw me, and 'e gave a funny flippin' grin, 'ard like, and I could see plain as kiss-me-arse what 'e was thinkin'. 'E was saying to 'imself,

'"There y'are, yer yeller bastards: take that lot for old Wilkie, and may you roast in 'ell, you shower o' stinkin' sods".'

Rogers looked round the Mess.

'That's what 'e was thinkin', plain as yer like. 'E'd been givin' 'em one for Wilkie, nothin' else.'

The words were hardly spoken when the klaxon roared over their heads, a blast as hard as a physical blow in its effect on the men who were sitting quiet and relaxed. The klaxon when the submarine was at periscope depth meant Collision Stations, shut off for depth-charging, dive to sixty feet. A bunch of half-a-dozen men performed the impossible feat of leaping aft through the bulkhead doorway in one solid mass: Shadwell heaved the door shut behind Chief Petty Officer Rawlinson as he fought his way in. The bar swung down, locking the heavy door in place.

Shadwell looked at Rawlinson, and put on his 'classy' voice:

'Excuse me, Mr Rawlinson, but have you any ideah what the flippin' 'ell's goin' on?'

The T.I. snapped: 'Get forward, help 'em shut off.' Shadwell lowered himself into the tube space, muttering fiercely.

In the Control Room, Number One watched the needle steady itself at the sixty mark.

'Sixty feet, sir.'

'Very good,' muttered the Captain. The submarine was going dead slow on one motor: overhead, two anti-submarine launches were searching for her. *Seahound* was on the wrong side of the entrance: she still had to get out.

'What was the seaplane doing, Number One, when you last saw it?'

'Circling over the harbour area, sir.'

The Captain thought: Perhaps the idiots think we're still hanging around at that end. Actually the submarine had been going her best speed towards the exit: a fairly obvious move, it would have seemed.

'Where are they now, Saunders?'

Saunders twiddled the wheel on his set: his ears looked so big that it might have been only the headphones that kept them from flapping.

'One right ahead, sir. Second one: I can't find the second one, sir. Must be stopped.'

The Captain glanced at the clock: dusk now, dark in an hour.

Saunders spoke: 'H.E., sir, right ahead, closing. Second H.E., sir, green two-oh. Closing, sir, moving slowly left to right.'

Those little bastards had to pass overhead: they had to pass overhead without detecting the submarine. God knows where they came from, the Captain thought: he hadn't any idea that there was anything of the sort in the area. He hoped there weren't any others in the bay.

Cat and mouse, creep quietly along, no sound, no sight. Eyes on Saunders: eyes on the Captain. The Captain turned to the Navigator at the chart table.

'There aren't any gun batteries on the point, are there, Pilot?'

'Nothing we know of, sir.' Was he thinking of trying to get out on the surface, with a Jap aircraft overhead?

Saunders looked up from the dial on his instrument.

'First one about to pass overhead, sir. Second one green seven-five, moving right.'

In the next five minutes they'd either pick up the submarine, or they'd have passed over and missed her. Engine-room Artificer Featherstone stared ruminatively up at the deckhead, as though he was trying to imagine the scene on the surface: he was wondering whether or not there'd be any charges dropped, in the next few minutes.

Saunders said, 'One passed over, sir, right astern, opening. Second one green nine-two, sir, moving right.'

The Captain turned to Number One.

'Sounds healthier,' he said. 'We'll keep on like this for an hour, then we'll surface and get out in the dark.'

'Aye aye, sir.' As long as something else didn't turn up, thought Number One, as long as those launches didn't come back again and pick them up.

Nothing else turned up. An hour later *Seahound* surfaced, left the bay at full speed on her diesels. Sub was on the bridge with the Captain: the land towered black over them on either side, fell away astern. They were out. The Captain said quietly,

'All right, Sub. I'll tell you when to come round to the new course.'

'Aye aye, sir.'

Just as the Captain joined Number One and the others in the Wardroom, they felt a series of heavy explosions. The Captain hurried back into the Control Room. 'What was that?' he asked the man who had relieved Saunders of the headphones.

'Right astern, sir. Depth-charges, I think.'

The Cox'n laughed. 'They must be dropping charges on some flippin' rock, sir.'

The Captain thought: Yes, or on poor old *Stringent*'s wreck. *Stringent* was the last submarine to have entered the Bay, and she'd been there ever since.

Is a man mad to talk to the stars, or, in the stillness of the empty night, to hold a conversation with the sea? When the sea leaps, and the stars are hidden, is he insane that he answers the thunder of the wind? Or is it possible that such things can be excused in a man who spends many hours alone, with only these for company?

He asks no man to excuse him, he offers no excuses for his actions. He knows that in the hand of the sea are the lives of men and the fate of nations, the happiness of millions and the future of the world. He knows also that under the sight of the stars the world was made, and in their light the miserable things called men are caused to be born, allowed mercifully to live and forced, struggling like frantic animals, to die. Between the sea and the stars, he has seen it.

The seaman's soul knows the vastness of the universe and the overwhelming savagery of forces that are uncaring of the suffering that they cause. He puts his trust in the things to which he owes allegiance. Do not laugh at the faith of such men, whose lives are bound in the ways of the elements: for if you do, you only snigger at yourselves and at your God.

CHAPTER FIVE

Stoker Johnson wiped the blade which he had just removed from his razor, and replaced it in the wrapper of blue paper. He stroked his large, smooth chin, admired it in the mirror on the wall of the after heads.

'Can't see why you all get so excited,' he remarked. 'Just because we're gettin' back to that bloody 'ole, Trinco, you act like a lot of flippin' kids off on 'oliday.'

Nobby Clark, the Leading Stoker, took his place at the basin and began to wash out the suds that Johnson had left in it.

'Well,' he said, 'it's better 'n being at sea, ain't it?'

'No it ain't, not to my way of thinking. At sea you know where you are, like: it ain't comfortable, but you don't expect the Ritz. You gets back to Trinco, and where are yer? Shouted at to do this an' that, no big eats, no flippin' room on the messdeck, queue up for a flippin' bath, clean the bugger up afterwards. An' what's the use o' going ashore in Trinco? You can swim better over the side. First time I goes ashore, I thinks to meself I'm going to 'ave a bit o' fun. What do I get? Flip-all, that's what. Not a woman in the 'ole flippin' area, and if you see one she's with an officer. An' mark you, Nobby, a man like me needs a woman.'

'Why you an' not me?'

'Well, I'm married, see. An' my wife 'as what you might call an appetite. So I'm used to it. Flippin' well need it, see? Not like you single bastards, take it when it's there an' forget it when it ain't. I'm used to 'avin' it when I want it, nice an' regular, see? Trinco: blimey, I'd be chasing the flippin' monkeys if we were in longer 'n a couple o' weeks.'

In the bar of the Depot Ship's wardroom, Number One and the Sub looked at their empty glasses and called for two more pink gins.

On the way in from patrol, everyone thinks the same thing: early night, turn in straight after dinner. But the first thing that comes is a bath, and the bath makes a difference. It washes off the smell of shale oil, eases out the tiredness in your body and your mind. You lie back in the bath, and sing: there are four baths in the bathroom, so it's quite a big sing. In the course of it, you forget the early night plan and you develop a thirst. As soon as you've changed, feel clean and smart after a long time of feeling dirty and unkempt, you find yourself quenching that thirst in the bar, one foot on the brass rail and a glass in your hand that has something in common with the widow's cruse.

'The Seahounds are back! Party tonight, boys!'

'We're turning in early.'

'The two of you, dears?'

'Tiny, if you want a kick where it hurts, just say that again.'

'I've been kicked there so often that it doesn't hurt any more. Now, what am I going to have?'

'A baby, by the look of you.' The remark came from Arthur Hallet, who had just entered the bar with two other C.O.'s. Tiny, who was certainly on the large size, murmured to Number One,

'You know, I don't think I like your Captain very much.'

'You don't? Well, that's all right. You don't have to.'

'What do you mean?'

'I mean as long as you keep any criticisms to yourself.'

'Oh. Like that, is it?'

'It's like that, Tiny.'

The bar was filling up as the bathrooms and cabins emptied themselves. A few odd pieces of soap clung to the soap-racks, discarded shirts and shorts littered the empty cabins. Below, in the cabin and bathroom flats, the singing was over.

'Hello, Jimmy! Wotcher, John! Sink anything?'

'Nothing much. Only half the Imperial Navy.'

'Both junks, eh. But what did you really get?' They told him.

'Not bad for beginners. Steward – gin bottle, please.'

After dinner, the Sub read the letters that had been waiting for him. It was a routine, well established, to save them for the quiet after-dinner period. First he read the ones from his family, then the one from the girl in Sussex, but he kept to the last the one and only letter addressed in Sheila's neat handwriting. He finished his black coffee, put the cup down and tore open the blue envelope. This was a thing that he had looked forward to doing.

Not what he'd hoped to read, though. She told him that she was engaged to Gerry Watson, and that she didn't think he ought to see her again. It would be better, she suggested, if he didn't spend another leave in Kandy.

The Sub could only agree with that. He knew that he wouldn't be able to face Kandy without Sheila. He thought of the lake, and knew that the affection which he had developed for it and for all the strange atmosphere of the place was only an offshoot of the way he felt about Sheila. Quickly he thought, that's nonsense: I've learnt a lesson, that's all.

As he sat there, opposite the big tray with the cups on it, a Medical Officer came along for his coffee. This was not only a doctor: this was the flotilla's psychoanalyst, the man who put chaps back on the rails when they had begun to go a little bit queer.

The doctor paused, lingering over the array of cups. There were white ones, and a minority which bore a floral design around the edges. He picked up one of these coloured ones, and stared towards the coffee-urn. Suddenly he whirled round, dropped the cup back on the tray as though it had burnt his fingers. He took one of the white ones instead, and smiled cautiously at the Sub who was watching in astonishment.

'I can't stand the ones with little pictures on them,' said the doctor.

After the late News from London, the B.B.C. orchestra played the National Anthem.

There were only a handful of men left in the bar: the Seahounds, a couple of other submarine officers and an R.N.V.R. Sub-Lieutenant whose green stripe marked him as non-executive, an officer whose duties confined him to an office where he ciphered and deciphered secret signals. The Anthem ended, and the young man said,

'Lot of tripe.'

'I beg your pardon?' asked Sub, and Number One rose to his feet.

'This King business,' said the Cipher Officer. 'It's out of date. What do we need a King for?'

The others were also on their feet. It was a long distance from the wardroom deck to the water-level, a very long drop indeed. They came back into the bar, and Jimmy suggested a nightcap. While the steward poured it out, Jimmy lifted the receiver off the intercom telephone.

'Quartermaster's Lobby,' he said to the exchange.

'Quartermaster? An officer has just fallen overboard on the port side. You'd better send a boat round. Yes, that's right. He may have broken his neck.'

The next afternoon they went swimming from a beach called Sweat Bay. It was fifteen minutes' walk from where the boat dropped them, through the trees where the monkeys lived, across a neck of land to the wide sweep of fine white sand on the other side.

Sub had brought a fitted charge, and when they were tired of swimming it was thrown into the water, as far out as possible. It went off like a miniature depth-charge, and they dived in to collect the stunned fish. Tiny made a fire of driftwood on the beach, and they baked the fish for tea. The meal tasted of mud and raw fish.

Number One spat out a lot of bones, and said,

'What about a run ashore tonight, Sub?'

'All right. Where?'

'Officers' Club, I suppose. Coming, Tiny?'

'Not me. Waste of money.' Tiny looked bigger than ever when he had nothing on.

'Oh, I wouldn't say that. There's liquor in the bar, and there are usually some women to look at.'

'Yes, at a distance, and that only makes it worse. Our own bar is all I want, and what's more it's Duty Free. Besides, there's not so far to walk, when you feel like turning in.'

They caught a boat for the shore after a couple of quick gins in the bar, and at the landing-stage they engaged a ricksha to pull them along to the Club. They ordered drinks on the verandah, sat next to a party of four people, two Naval officers and two Wrens. Jimmy waved and smiled at one of the girls, and she discreetly returned the greeting. She was small, blonde, bright-looking: she had a snub nose in a well made-up face. She reminded the Sub of some Hollywood girl who had a raucous voice and a big mouth: he couldn't remember the name. He asked Number One who the girl was.

'Mary-Ann. Her surname's Chard. She was Smiley Martin's girl-friend: he's just gone home, you know. I'll have a chat to her later: she shouldn't be seen out with General Service chaps. It's not respectable.'

After dinner they drank in the bar on the ground-floor. Jimmy said,

'Excuse me a minute, old boy.'

'Going to be sick?'

'No. Going to talk to Mary-Ann.'

Twenty minutes later he came back, looking pleased with himself.

'Sorry, Sub. Couldn't get away.'

Sub had been talking to someone in the bar, or rather the other fellow had been doing the talking and Sub had pretended to be listening while he drank his drink and thought about Sheila.

'Submarines!' said the man. 'What on earth, now, do people join submarines for?' He went on to answer his own question at considerable length, and Sub thought about the real answer in his own case.

Well, his first ship had been a battleship in the Mediterranean, an unusual sort of battleship because it had a damn great hole in it. An Italian submarine had done that: a midget submarine controlled by only two men had put one of the mightiest ships afloat out of action for months. It gave him a strange, exciting impression of the power that a few men hold in their hands. Seeing the submarines in the harbour at Alexandria he felt again that impression of swift, ruthless power, and it captured his imagination. The submarines lay alongside each other, amongst the rest of the fleet, and he saw them suddenly with the eyes of a submariner. They were wolves, amongst dogs.

So he joined them. But he couldn't explain that sort of thing to a half-drunken bore who only raised the subject to give himself something to talk about. He wouldn't understand, even if he'd listen. Sub couldn't explain it any more than he could explain how much Sheila had meant to him. The only thing that a man like this would really feel would be a kick in the belly. He thought, Odd, that's how I feel, like I'd just been kicked in the belly by a horse. But only now, he thought, because I'm a bit tight. In the morning, it won't matter.

Jimmy's glass was empty, so he finished his own and addressed the barman.

'Two brandy and sodas, please.'

Golf at Nuwara Eliya was played on a course which was far from easy to the uninitiated: streams criss-crossed the terrain in numbers to rival the streams of the Nile delta, and the streams were by no means as sluggish as the waterways of that insanitary area. These ran fast, in some places torrentially: golf balls, one after the other, vanished into their crystal depths. The caddies, small coffee-coloured urchins, had so many repaints ready to hand that it seemed not unlikely that secret pools or backwaters were the sources of their raw material.

Chief and the Captain were short-tempered long before they ended the round, and when they limped into the clubhouse in search of the watery tasteless beer which was all the bar stocked, and the elderly stranger who wore the uniform of a Captain in the Pioneer Corps addressed them in terms of some familiarity, it was perhaps pardonable that Chief's reaction was more brusque than might have been expected from an officer from the cream of the Senior Service.

' 'Ullo, Jack!'

'My name,' growled Chief, 'is not Jack.'

'Jack's good enough for me. Any Navy lad's Jack to me. Care for a spot?'

'All right. Thanks.'

'Boy, three glasses o' that yellow stuff. Beer, is it?' The man's thin bony knees looked cold in their whiteness, and his hands trembled where they rested on the edge of the bar. He suggested:

'Tell y' a story?'

'No, thanks,' answered Chief.

'Listen, boy, I got some stories 'd make y' hair curl. Sure, I have. The real McCoy. I been around, I have. Ah, the beer, my boys, the beer it is to be sure!'

'Excuse me,' put in Chief. 'Forgive a personal question. But a moment ago you were speaking in an American accent, and shortly before that it was Cockney. Now it's Irish. Where do you come from?'

'Oh, I been around. Sure, I been all over. Tell y' about it: drink first.'

'They've got a nerve to call this stuff beer,' observed the Captain, lowering his glass.

'Tell y' what I call it,' offered the Pioneer. 'Horse-piss.'

Chief shook his head. 'It can't be horse,' he argued. 'I've had that: it's what they call beer in Egypt. This is quite different.'

'Some other sort. Elephant, eh?'

'Can't be elephant. That'd be stronger. Something else.'

'Snake? Ah, that's it! Snake! Boy – three more from the old snake. Then I'll tell 'y all about it. I'm up from C'lombo. Terrible.'

'I've heard it's rather nice.'

'Nice? Boy, it's all loose women! Looser 'n you've ever set eyes on. I tell y', I'm here for a rest. Couldn't stand it! At me all day, they were. Terrible. A man like me doesn't stand a chance. Not a chance!' He was excited, the veins swelling blue on his white temples: he swept out his arm in a violent gesture that threw his glass off the counter: the crash coincided with the opening of the clubhouse door. An ambulance man beckoned to the Pioneer.

'Come along now, sir.' The voice was quiet, assured in its power of command. 'Come along, sir.'

'He wants to take me away!' The thin figure detached itself from the bar, stood hesitant, rather bent, eyes darting to and from the man in the doorway. His whole body shook, not only his hands.

'Wants to take me away!' he repeated, more loudly, staring crazily at Chief. His face began to crumple like a child's before the tears, and while the ambulance man stood there watching and the barman slowly wiped the counter the Pioneer's feet edged forward towards the door that stood open to receive him. The barman picked up a glass that was already clean, frowned at it while he twirled it in the towel.

Chief pushed away his unfinished drink.

'Jesus Christ!' he muttered. 'There are worse things than war...'

Number One and the Sub faced each other across the wardroom table. They sat with their feet up on the lockers, for the battery boards that formed the deck had been removed to allow the electricians to top up the cells of the battery with distilled water.

The Sub said,

'There's a dance tonight, at the Club. Wish to God there were some more women in this blasted place.'

Number One smiled. 'I'm going to ring up Mary-Ann.' He was still smiling to himself as he climbed across the framework of the deck and went into the Control Room. Smiley Martin had been a fly in the ointment for many months. Kneeling down, he cracked a joke with the Leading Electrician as he examined the top of a cell: he was looking forward to tonight.

Sub thought for a moment, undecided. He reached for a cigarette and was about to strike a match when he remembered that the battery was open: no smoking. The unlit cigarette in his mouth, he went for'ard, up the ladder and over the plank, up the long gangway into the Depot Ship. In the wardroom entrance he lit his cigarette, then picked up the phone and asked to be connected with the Wrennery.

'Mary-Ann? This is John Ferris. Sub of *Seahound*. Yes, I met you once at a party, with Smiley.... Look, is anyone taking you to the dance tonight? ... That's marvellous! ... Can I pick you up at the Wrennery? – about seven? ... Fine. See you then.' He rang off, went back to work.

In the submarine, Number One looked at him and asked,

'What are you looking so pleased with yourself about?'

'Oh, nothing. Just my usual cheerful self.' He thought for the first time: This is going to be a little awkward by and by. It was a dirty trick, but he consoled himself with the idea that love and war justified any extraordinary behaviour.

'Isn't it about time to knock off?'

Number One looked at him. 'No, not for another half-hour. If you've nothing to do I can give you plenty.'

'Oh, I've lots to do, thanks. I'm thirsty, that's all.'

'Are you ever not thirsty?' Sub ignored the question, went for'ard to talk to Rawlinson.

At lunchtime he was drinking quietly in the bar with Tiny, when he heard his name almost shouted from a distance of about a couple of feet. It was his First Lieutenant, scarlet in the face.

'Come with me.' He followed Number One out of the wardroom.

'Sub, you're required on board as Duty Officer tonight and every night for a week. I think you've been getting rather above yourself.'

'Damn it, Number One! You can't do that! ... I've got a date tonight, in any case.'

'No, you haven't. I've explained that you'd forgotten you were Duty. She quite understood. I'll be looking after her. You're Duty for a week, and if there's any argument you can see the Commander, now. All right?'

'All right.' You couldn't always be clever, he thought. He moved back into the bar, and Tiny gave him a gin.

'Trouble?' asked Tiny.

'Oh, no. Cheers.' Seven days on board, in this heat. It was largely the fault of the heat, anyway. And there was Sheila, or rather the lack of her.

Next day, at about six-thirty, Number One and Tiny were drinking the inevitable pink gin in the bar of the Depot Ship, when Sub strolled in. He had been loading torpedoes into *Seahound*'s tubes all afternoon, which had been a hot and tiring

100

way of spending an afternoon when it was too hot even to light a cigarette without regretting the extra heat of the match.

'Hello, John,' called Tiny. 'What'll it be?'

'Pinkers, please.'

Jimmy asked him, 'Don't you ever do any drinking in the accommodation ship?'

'Oh, yes. When I'm not Duty.'

'Run two wine bills, I suppose?'

'Sh!' Sub had seen the Commander of the flotilla enter the bar. The Commander had an Army major with him, and they ordered drinks at the other end of the long bar. It wasn't often that guests were seen in this ship, and Army men were like men from Mars. It was almost a surprise to see that they drank like other people. The Commander looked round, and his eye rested for a long moment on the junior officers. Number One had a nasty feeling that he was about to be informed of something wrong in the appearance of his submarine: the Ensign not flying free, perhaps, some gear left on the casing.

'You *Seahound* people. Come here.'

Number One and the Sub dutifully left Tiny and approached the two at the other end.

'Evening, sir,' said Number One.

'Evening. Want you to meet these young fellows, Major. Lieutenant Wentworth, Sub-Lieutenant Ferris, of the *Seahound*. Major Worth.' The Major was a hard-looking soldier with a bayonet scar on his cheek.

They shook hands, and the Commander ordered fresh drinks. He said to the Major, 'I'm afraid Lieutenant Commander Hallet won't be back off leave for another week or so. But you'll have plenty of time to get to know each other.'

Later, Sub said to Number One, 'Looks like we're taking the Army to sea, this time.'

'A very clever deduction. God damn it: I hate these Special Operations.'

'Why? Makes a change.'

'A hell of a change. Overcrowded in the wardroom, then an operation that's likely to be bloody dangerous and not even a sinking to show for it. I wonder if the Old Man knows about this?'

'Come to think of it, I reckon he does. He said something about not taking any reload torpedoes, this patrol.'

'Not any?'

'No, just the six in the tubes. That means canoes, I suppose.'

'Yes. Several canoes. And that means it's not only the Major, but all his pals as well. Christ, why does it have to be us?'

The Captain and Chief were having a party in the small lounge of their hotel. There were the two of them, and two girls: one was a Wren officer, the other an American. They were drinking, and dancing to a radiogram that had seen better days. The Captain had taken first claim on the American girl, and the Chief had the Wren.

Late in the evening, as they put the corks back in the bottles, the Captain made a suggestion.

'Let's climb the mountain tomorrow, shall we?'

Chief groaned. 'It's a hell of a long way up,' he said.

'Sure!' The Captain's girl-friend approved. 'Let's go up that Ragalla, or whatever they call it. O.K., Jean?'

'Why, yes. It'll do us all good,' agreed the Wren, looking at Chief. He winced.

Next morning after breakfast they were given a lift in an Army car up to where the slopes steeped towards the wooded mountain, and from that point the climb began. It was not really a climb, but more of a steep uphill walk.

Three-quarters of an hour later, the American girl stumbled: the Captain grabbed her, held her up.

'Wow!' she shrieked. 'That was my ankle! Guess I'll have to take your arm from here on, Arthur boy.'

Chief and Jean kept well ahead after that. The Captain said, 'Those two seem to be hitting it off pretty well.'

Sal laughed. 'Jean's in love with the Navy,' she said. 'I guess if she married one of you fellers she'd hang the guy over the back of a chair and hop into bed with the uniform.'

She was leaning her weight on him, and she leant with her body half-turned to his. She knew all about her figure, and she liked to see the effect it had on him. She herself was not un-moved.

Chief and Jean were a good thirty yards ahead.

'Honey,' murmured Sal, 'I guess we don't have to get to the top of this darned hill, do we? How about we wait here and let them go ahead?'

The Captain shouted to Chief,

'You two go on. Sal's ankle's bad. We'll see you on your way down.'

Stumbling through a short stretch of forest they came to an open space, the forest behind them and a drop of a thousand feet in front.

Sal laid her long body down: the Captain stood for a moment, looking down into the valley.

'Honey,' she said, 'I need some comfort for my ankle.'

His week of penance over, Sub joined the others in the afternoon boat ashore: they took the Major to Sweat Bay, and taught him their own game of 'submarines'. For this game it was essential to have Tiny in the party, since his size made him an ideal 'convoy'. The others split up into two teams, one of which formed the escort for the convoy and the other a wolfpack of submarines. The convoy had to proceed from one fixed point to another, and was allowed to zigzag or to make emergency turns, which it signalled in the correct manner to its escorts. The submarines submerged ahead or around the convoy and endeavoured to surface underneath it after avoiding the screen of escorts. To claim a sinking it was necessary to strike the target in its belly: a submarine was sunk when an escort managed to tread on it.

The Major proved to be an excellent submarine, having a remarkable endurance under water and a very accurate aim at close quarters. After three or four attacks the convoy begged to be excused, on the grounds that it was waterlogged.

'I'm afraid we're going to crowd you out rather, in your little wardroom,' remarked the Major.

'Won't be too bad there,' the Captain told him. 'Two of your officers on hammock mattresses on the deck, under the table, and one in the Control Room. You'll have a bunk, of course, and my officers will have to work 'hot bunks'. Every bunk full all the time, you see, but one man always on watch. When he comes off watch he turns in to the bunk his relief came out of.'

'I see. Can't be very pleasant when it's hot.'

'Oh, you get used to it. But the Petty Officers' Mess will be a bit crowded, I'm afraid, with your four sergeants. Can't be helped.'

The party was to consist of the Major, three other officers and four sergeants. Four canoes were to be stowed in the racks where normally the spare torpedoes were kept. Each canoe would be manned by one officer and one sergeant. The three officers and the sergeants were due to arrive next morning, before they sailed.

'Well,' remarked the Captain, 'you can keep your job. I'll stay in my nice safe submarine.'

'Oh, nonsense. My job sounds a lot more dangerous than it is.'

'It'll be a good subject for a book, after the war.'

'When the war's over, people won't want to read about it. Not for a few years, anyway. As a matter of fact. I have tried writing a few things, but the only really good things that I've produced have been after a lot of whisky. That's all right, but it gets better and better until I can't read what I've written. I wouldn't be surprised if the world had lost a number of literary masterpieces that way.'

They were sailing next day. In the flotilla, people pretended not to notice the soldiers, their equipment, weapons and canoes. It was all very hushed, and nobody knew anything about it. The monkeys were interested, though: from the bow of the Depot Ship a long cable ran to a palm-tree on the shore, and in the cool of the evenings the monkeys used to sit on it, swing by their feet and dip their hands in the water. When they saw the canoes being lowered one by one into the submarine's for'ard hatch, they danced and gibbered more than ever.

CHAPTER SIX

Able Seaman Rogers divested himself of his shorts, and stared with considerable disfavour at the canoes which lined the bulkheads of the for'ard Mess. It was not that they took up any more room than the torpedoes which normally occupied the racks, but the mere fact that this was something different and slightly foreign to the normally accepted routine of submarining.

'And where the flippin' 'ell are we taking these flippin' punts to?' he asked his messmates. Seeing them there was like being handed a cup of coffee when he'd asked for a cuppo'.

'We'll know, soon enough,' muttered Parrot. 'Don't make much odds, do it?'

Rogers looked sternly at him. 'I like to know what I'm flippin' well doing,' he said.

'Well,' put in Shadwell, 'what about puttin' something over yer nasty looking be'ind, for a start?'

There was a click and a humming noise as the broadcasting system was switched on from the Control Room. Rogers quickly pulled on a pair of dirty overalls.

'D'you hear there? D'you hear there?' came the Captain's voice.

'We can 'ear,' muttered Rogers.

'We have on board a party of military personnel. We are going to land them, in about a week's time, on a Jap beach. The job they have to do will take them about two days to complete. After that time we'll pick 'em up again.

'Now, listen. This is the biggest thing we've ever done. I can't go into details, but I can tell you that it's absolutely vital. We can only do it properly and come home again if every man in the ship's company does his job with one hundred per cent efficiency. One slip, and we've had it. I'm not doubting the ability of any of you. I'm only telling you that if you've ever been on your toes, you've got to be now.

'We're honoured in being given this job. Every one of us. You all know that up to now we've been limited as to how far down the Straits we can go. Well, the limit's off. We're going through the minefields. We'll be closer to Singapore than any of His Majesty's Ships has been since we lost the place. And what our Army friends are going to do down there is going to hurt the bloody Nips more than they've been hurt for a long time. That's all.'

The broadcast switched off, and Rogers buttoned up his trousers.

'Thanks for the bleedin' honour,' he said.

Number One was standing in the Control Room, looking disgruntled, when Sub dropped off the ladder beside him.

'Look here, Sub,' he said, pointing to the grey tin boxes of Oerlikon ammunition which Rogers had stowed in the corner by the helmsman's seat. 'We can't have all your department's rubbish in the Control Room, you know.'

'Sorry, Number One. But where the hell can we stow it? The magazine's full, we can't put another sausage for'ard: poor buggers haven't got room to spit as it is with all those bloody tommy-guns and things.'

'That's your worry. Get this stuff out of here, now.'

'God blast all First Lieutenants,' thought the Sub. He was careful not to voice the thought. He shouted,

'Rogers in the Control Room!'

'Want me, sir?' Rogers had been standing behind him.

'Oh. Yes, get these boxes of ammo out of here. Find some other place for them.'

'Blimey,' muttered Rogers. He set off for'ard again, peering into corners which were all full of something.

Presently the Gunlayer came along. 'Sir: them boxes of Oerlikon. I could put 'em down below by the magazine, but the Engineer's gear 's all down there.'

'Oh, it is, is it? Well, put it out, and put these boxes down there instead.'

'Aye aye, sir.'

Sub joined the crowd in the wardroom. There certainly wasn't much room to spare. The Major introduced him: Captain Selby, Captain Bowers, Lieutenant Montgomery.

'Any relation to the man in the black beret?'

'None at all. I don't even like being photographed.'

The Chief Engine-room Artificer spoke from the gangway.

'Engineer Officer, sir?'

'Oh, hell. Yes, Chatterley?'

'It appears, sir, that the Gunlayer 'as thrown our stuff out of the machinery space 'ere. According to 'is orders, 'e says.'

'Sub!'

'Hello, Chiefy.'

'You can tell him to put it all back, if you value your skin.'

'I don't. And I can't. That's my stowage space. Look at the orders.'

'And where the hell do you expect me to put my stuff?'

'Wherever you bloody well like, old boy.'

'I'll see Number One about this.'

'Do. That's where I started from. Ask him if you can put it in the Control Room. There's an empty corner by the helmsman.'

Chief lurched away to find Number One. The Chief E.R.A. followed him, shaking his head sadly.

'Do any of you play bridge?' asked Captain Bowers, who had taken some cards out of his pack and was shuffling them quietly in the corner.

'No,' answered the Sub. 'Don't get time. We play Liar Dice, mostly.'

'Never heard of it.'

'You'll soon learn.' Sub thrust his hand into a pigeon-hole in the correspondence locker and brought out five ivory dice. He threw them on the table.

'Look. Same hands as for Poker, you see...' The Army gathered round....

Sub was on watch at night, the silence of the empty sky and sea far more noticeable than the noise of both diesels turning over at three hundred and eighty revolutions to the minute. The sky was a velvet cushion, studded with stars, the sea a mirror of black glass. The sharp bow cut into it, spoiling the unbroken trackless water as a pair of skis can lacerate the smooth side of a mountain.

'Relieve lookout, sir?'

'Yes, please.'

He was thinking about his job in this landing business. Being the officer responsible for everything that happened on the casing, the steel deck on top of the submarine's hull, it was his job to handle and launch the canoes. It had to be done quickly and quietly, in the dark, with the submarine trimmed down low so that the for'ard hatch was only just clear of the water. This put the submarine in a position to dive quickly if an emergency arose, reduced her silhouette and made the canoe-launching easier.

Luckily the sea was certain to be dead flat, down there where the Straits were narrower than some rivers. The for'ard hatch had to be open for the least possible time, for while it was open she could not dive. The canoes had to be hauled out one by one and launched over the side, steadied while their crews climbed into them, pushed off. Four canoes: it would take about five minutes, in the dark, within pistol shot of an enemy beach.

Sub only had that little part of the business to worry about. The Captain, down below in the wardroom, had very much more. If the enemy had the slightest clue that they were down there, he could just as well write his ship off. Within an hour of some little slip giving away their position, an Escort Group would be steaming out of Singapore. In the narrow waters there could be no question of escape. Anything could give them away. Six inches too much periscope, seen from the shore. A slight noise when they were dived, picked up on a Japanese hydrophone. A chance meeting with a patrol boat ... and in any case, they had first to get through the minefield, a minefield that had not been passed since the day it was laid.

The Captain was having a conference with the Major. The wardroom table was covered by the chart of the area, military maps and aerial photographs taken by reconnaissance planes within the last few weeks.

The object of the operation on shore was as much a mystery to the Captain as it was to everyone else, except of course to the Army men, and of them only the Major knew the full details. Until the time came when they had to know, just before they landed, he told them nothing. The fewer that knew anything, the less chance there was of the Japs knowing. The submarine could be sunk, and the survivors taken prisoner, and the Japanese had many ways of extracting information from prisoners. Even the bravest had been known to talk, at about the time that they went out of their minds.

'Y' know,' observed the Major, 'we're all going to find life damned monotonous, when this war ends.'

'I should think you probably will,' agreed the Captain.

'No, damn it, you as well: won't you?'

'Perhaps, at first. But even in peace-time the Navy offers a certain amount of excitement.'

'I suppose it depends on the way you look at it,' mused the soldier.

'I was regular, you know: chucked it up. Couldn't stand all the social nonsense. All the wives saying Yes sir, No sir, to each other, according to their husband's ranks. Damn it, if I marry a girl, it doesn't make her a Major!'

'It could be pretty frightful,' murmured Number One, thoughtfully. The Major turned to him.

'I was stationed in Malta, at one time. My Colonel's wife went to have her hair done in a place that had little sort of booths, all partitioned off. On each side of her, behind the partitions, was a Naval officer's wife. They must have thought the place between them was empty, because one of them suddenly said across to the other, "My deah, have you chosen your soldiah for the summah?"'

'Good Lord! That can't be normal, can it?'

'Well, you see, in the summer the fleet used to leave Malta on a summer cruise. Chaps had a whale of a time on the Riviera, and all that sort of thing.'

Number One was very thoughtful, still. The Captain grinned at him.

'Worried, Number One?'

'No, sir, I'm not worried. But I've thought about it quite a bit, and I don't think I'll stay in the Navy after the war, not if they'll let me out.'

'You're not serious?'

'Yes, I am. I'm enjoying this war, and I like my job, and all that sort of thing. But in peace-time I'd be bored stiff. I'm sure of it.'

'You'll get used to it, when it comes. And in any case, if it's anything like the last one we'll all be damn lucky if we aren't thrown out when they start disarming.... Let's have the dice out: like a game, Major?' The soldier said he would.

'Right. Ace up, King towards, spin for start ... yours, Number One.'

The Navigator finished his tea and squeezed himself out of the wardroom, went into the Control Room and addressed the helmsman,

'Relief O.O.W.,' he said. The helmsman shouted up the voice-pipe,

'Relieve Officer of the Watch, sir?'

'Yes, please.' The answer came out of the brass tube in Number One's voice. The Navigator climbed the ladder to the bridge, took over the watch.

'O.K., Tommy. Course 100 degrees, three-eight-oh revs. There's the land.' Number One pointed at the Northern end of Sumatra: they were approaching the top of the Straits, and next morning at dawn they would be diving.

Number One slid down the ladder to his tea. Somehow they managed to make room for him round the table: it seemed that you could always get in one more, however many there were already. He had finished his tea and was just lighting a match, when the klaxon gave a preliminary cough and then roared twice. The soldiers sat in stunned surprise at the violent, lightning evacuation. The Major went on drinking his tea.

'What's all this in aid of?' asked Selby.

'Don't ask me. Perhaps they're issuing rum, or something. Pass the sugar, would you, Montgomery?'

As the Navigator fell into the Control Room on top of the Lookout, he said,

'Aircraft, sir, coming towards from right ahead.'

'Sixty feet,' ordered the Captain. Five minutes later, he

changed the order.

'Thirty feet, Number One.'

'Thirty feet, sir.' The submarine rose gently to periscope depth, thirty feet, and the Captain signalled with his hands for the periscope to be raised. Slowly, carefully, he searched the sky.

'Nothing there, now.' He stepped back, turned to Number One as the periscope hissed down.

'We'll stay dived until dark. Go to Watch Diving when you're ready.'

'Aye aye, sir. Which Watch, Cox'n?'

'White Watch, sir.' Number One lifted the microphone down from its hook.

'White Watch, Watch Diving.'

Silence settled heavily through the compartments as the routine ticked along like a clock and the submarine began to creep into the Straits.

'Mean to say we're going to stay under water for four hours, now?' asked the Major. 'Sounds most unhealthy to me.'

The Captain grinned. 'While you're disporting yourselves on the beach, or wherever you are going to disport yourselves, we'll be lying under water for forty-eight hours.'

Number One, who had just joined them in the wardroom, whistled.

'D'you mean that, sir?'

'Of course I mean it. We'll lie on the bottom all the time. Won't be able to run the air-conditioning plant: makes too much bloody noise. It'll be a bit hot, I dare say.'

'Hot! Good God, we'll bloody well fry!' Chief moaned, and began to wipe the soles of his feet with a towel.

All around them was the thick, black curtain of the night, in their ears the low throb of the diesels. In the front of the bridge stood the Captain and the First Lieutenant, their binoculars at their eyes, silently intent, watching to pick up the first glimpse of the lighthouse on the One Fathom Bank.

'Should see it any minute, now,' muttered the Captain. The lighthouse had no light in it, of course: only a tall, lonely pillar rising out of the middle of the Straits, a sign that here was the Bank, and beyond it a channel that twisted through countless other banks. The channel that was mined.

Minutes passed slowly as they strained their eyes ahead, occasionally taking the glasses from their eyes for long enough to blink before resuming the search.

'There it is, sir.' Number One spoke quietly, as though not wishing to break the clinging silence. The time was five-thirty.

'Good,' said the Captain, when he picked up the dark silhouette in his glasses. 'We're right on the dot, Number One. Hold this course until I shout up, then come round to one-two-oh and go slow together. I want to get a Radar fix, if I can.'

'Aye aye, sir.' As the Captain's dark form merged into the hatch, Number One spoke to the Lookout. 'Keep your eyes skinned.'

In twenty minutes' time they would be diving, and by eight o'clock they would be among the mines. Number One was hungry: he wondered what was for breakfast.

Saunders, his ears held into his head by the headphones, sat in the corner of the Control Room and operated the machine that could detect the presence of mines. The submarine was just entering the area which was marked off on the chart in red ink, shaded with diagonal lines and marked, simply, MINEFIELD. Saunders' long unshaven face was quite expressionless as he turned the handle in front of him, stared at the dial and lived through his ears. He would have worn exactly the same expression, or lack of one, if he had been operating a plough, intent on keeping the furrow straight and true.

Every eye in the Control Room was, most of the time, on Saunders' face. He seemed unconscious of the part he was playing. Nobody made a sound, nobody moved an inch. The sweat ran down: no hand was raised to wipe it off. The First Lieutenant stood with his back to the ladder, his eyes fixed on the depth-gauge in which the needle never moved. The Navigator leaned over the chart table, a pencil poised four inches above the word MINEFIELD. It had been poised, in exactly that position, for seven and a half minutes. The Sub was in the for'ard compartment with Chief Petty Officer Rawlinson and the torpedomen: they sat in silence, looking at their feet. The submarine had been shut off for depth-charging, which meant amongst other things that all the watertight doors were shut. Each compartment was a world on its own, linked to the Control Room by telephone. In the Engine-room, Chief leant against the port diesel, his eyes fixed without expression on a wheel-spanner that hung from an overhead pipe.

In the Control Room, nobody had moved. Saunders drew in his breath, sharply, and the Captain, looking at him, raised his eyebrows in a wordless question.

'Mine, right ahead.'

'Starboard ten.' The Captain's voice was low, unhurried. The course was altered by fifteen degrees.

'Mine, five degrees on the starboard bow.'

'Port ten.' *Seahound* turned back again by five degrees, to pass between the mines.

Featherstone raised his right hand from his side, stared at his fingernails. Everyone saw him do it. He seemed to find the thumb particularly interesting. The Signalman, irritated, looked at him angrily, and Featherstone dropped his hand to his side. The Signalman stared at his feet.

The Captain said, 'Report all objects.'

Saunders nodded, turned his wheel. His ears, Featherstone saw for the first time, were much bigger than the headphones.

'Contact, red three-one.' He turned the wheel a little more, and he added, 'Contact, green two-eight.'

'Very good.'

The Signalman looked up at the deckhead, pursed his lips as though he was whistling. Featherstone glared at him: the Signalman's lips relaxed and he stared at the hairs on the back of the First Lieutenant's neck.

'Mine, right ahead.'

The Navigator dropped his pencil. It made a mark on the charted minefield as the Captain asked,

'Where are the other two, now?'

'Red four-eight, sir.' Pause. 'Green three-seven.'

'Very good.' The Captain relapsed into silence, rubbing his chin. The helmsman waited tensely for an alteration of course.

None had been ordered. He had heard Saunders report a mine right ahead. The helmsman felt sweat running fast down his back.

The Captain spoke to Saunders.

'Tell me when the one to port bears red six-oh.'

'Aye aye, sir.'

They were all staring at the Captain, willing him to alter course. He looked at nobody except at Saunders.

Each minute took an hour to pass. Saunders raised his head, opened his mouth. The Captain's eyes brightened, and his face asked the question. Saunders closed his mouth again, twiddled his wheel a little bit this way and that. The Navigator looked at his pencil: the point was broken, so he put it down and picked up another one. That was broken, too. That seemed terribly funny: it took an effort not to laugh aloud.

Featherstone, watching the Captain and Saunders, felt like giggling himself. He didn't know why.

Saunders said, 'Red six-oh, sir. Second contact right ahead, still. And – green five-four.'

The Captain jerked his eyes to the man at the wheel. He snapped:

'Port ten.' He had coloured slightly, as though he was embarrassed. His were not the only eyes that watched the helmsman's indicator as it showed the submarine's swing from the old course. The relief was plain on many faces.

Saunders spoke again,

'Mine, right ahead. . . .'

In the wardroom, in utter silence, the Major and his three officers were reading books. They must have been books of considerable interest, for each of them seemed completely absorbed. Elbows on the table, heads in their hands, they presented a picture of static concentration that would have been an easy target for a sculptor.

The Major turned over a page too quickly, and they were all aware of the sound it made. They had grown used to the small sounds from the Control Room, the occasional report, the low orders. They could hear the tension.

114

Suddenly they heard the Captain's voice.

'Number One. Go to Watch Diving. Open up from depth-charging.'

Before the import of the order had broken through the taut minds all around him, the Captain was in the wardroom.

'We're through, Major,' he announced, quietly. 'Just in time for lunch.'

For the rest of that day, *Seahound* kept steadily on down the Straits. Amongst the ship's company, plain in every face and in the voices of the men as they went about their work or chatted during the off-watch spell, was a sense of elation, almost of victory. It came partly from relief, a reaction to the tense feelings of the morning, and partly from pride in having been the first ship to carry her flag so far down the dangerous passage. They had opened the door, and now, with their track clearly marked and inked on the chart, they knew that by following the same route exactly they or any other ship could do it again. The lock that had held for three years had been picked. There were other difficulties ahead, of course, but that only started tomorrow, and today, as Rogers put it, they had 'flippin' well done it'.

'Fair took me back, it did,' he mused. 'Back to the day me old man caught Ma with the chimney-sweep. Dead quiet, it was, all flippin' day. Me Dad didn't say nothin', nobody did. Come six o'clock he flipped off dahn the flippin' road to the local. Come back fair screechin', 'e did, an' laid into old Ma with a broom 'andle. She didn't 'alf carry on.'

Shadwell gazed at him, interest in his leathery face.

'Well!' he murmured. 'Never would 'a known you 'ad soot in y' blood.'

In the wardroom there was a similar tendency towards high spirits, but it was tempered with new purpose. The successful passage of the minefield galvanized the Major into violent activity: he knew now that there was no doubt about his operation taking place, and at once the charts, maps and photographs reappeared on the wardroom table. He and the Captain checked and rechecked distances and positions, drew up a timetable, tore it up and started on a new one. The Army officers went for'ard, and, with their sergeants, checked over their weapons and equipment. They were now the central figures in the operation: the submariners had played their part, or at any rate the hardest part of it; they had only to follow the thing through, keep their ship hidden, carry out the drill, land the soldiers and be in the right place to pick them up. That was all, but the Captain knew how easily everything could go wrong, and how suddenly.

The Major and his men were to be landed on the Malayan coast, South of Malacca. The spot chosen was the nearest point to Singapore at which it was considered possible to make a landing and get away unseen. It seemed logical to suppose that the soldiers were going into Singapore: but nobody knew, except for the Major, and neither the Captain nor any of the men who manned *Seahound* would ever know.

The Major sipped thoughtfully at his cup of dark brown tea. Once again his mind travelled over every detail, went back over each stage of the planning. No, he didn't think there could have been any leakage of information. If there had been – but that sort of thinking didn't get you anywhere. It only reminded him of a trip out of Haifa, a few years ago, a time when there had been a leakage. It reminded him of the cost that a leakage carried. Part of it had been his brother. The Major pulled himself together. He asked,

'D'you think I could have another cup?' Sub reached up and pressed the buzzer.

That evening they surfaced for the last night's dash. So close to the enemy, the Captain spent most of the night on the bridge with the Officers of the Watch, not because he had any lack of faith in their ability but because the responsibility was heavy on his shoulders and he found himself physically incapable of sitting down below. The watches changed quietly, peacefully, no incident of any sort while the enemy coast was plain in sight to starboard and to port, and just before dawn the Captain sent the Lookout and the Officer of the Watch down into the Control Room. He took a final look round, and dropped into the hatch, and shouted 'Dive, dive, dive!' so as not to make a noise by using the klaxon. He heard the roar of escaping air as the vents slammed down, and spray was falling on his head before he shut

116

the hatch. He jammed on the clips, climbed down into the Control Room. They had arrived, on schedule.

The day was spent making a periscope reconnaissance of the beach and its surroundings. The Captain and the Major spent most of the time in the Control Room. It was a strange sensation, this proximity to the enemy for whom they felt such a personal loathing. Meals in the wardroom were haphazard, social intercourse was disorganized by constant interruptions, by the necessity for searching through a heap of maps for the butter, or removing the chart to fix the position of a knife and fork. The soldiers were restless, more so after each had been given a long look at their landing-place: Captain Selby had lost his glasses, but he seemed perfectly at home without them.

The soldiers were a source of great interest to the submarine officers, who watched them and talked to them rather as prison warders might behave towards men condemned to the gallows. Nothing was too much trouble. The objects of their sympathetic interest, though obviously anxious for the dark hours to come, appeared unaffected by the imminence of what seemed at any rate to Chief to be a certain death. Chief made himself particularly helpful to the guests, continually making suggestions and offering friendly advice as to the best manner of handling canoes. He was a yachtsman himself, he explained, and he knew quite a bit about handling small craft. He left little doubt, in the course of his suggestions, that it would only be a one-way journey.

After tea they put the maps away, and the Captain, after a final talk with the Major, said,

'Right, Number One. We'll surface at nine-thirty. All canoes will be away by nine-fifty at the latest, and we'll dive again at about eleven. You can tell the hands.'

Supper was ready at six-thirty, finished and cleared away at seven. Number One pressed the buzzer for the messenger, sent for the Cox'n.

'Cox'n: tell the T.I. to have the for'ard Mess unrigged. Everything in the gangway and in the Leading Hands' Mess.'

'Aye aye, sir.' The Hands turned to, taking hammocks, kit-

117

bags, the table and everything movable out of the for'ard Mess.

At about eight, the Captain said,

'Sub. Get the canoes and tackles ready up for'ard.'

'Aye aye, sir.' Sub climbed for'ard over the heaps of gear that now littered the gangway. He found the for'ard compartment bare, except for some disconsolate seamen.

'Right. We'll get the canoes out of the racks. Shadwell: get the tackles ready.'

At half-past eight they were finished, the canoes lying on the deck ready to be hauled up to the hatch. A block was provided to be hooked on at the top of the hatchway, the rope already rove through it and one end of the rope, fitted with a spring-hook, secured to the bow of the first canoe. Sub looked round at the preparations.

'All right, T.I.,' he said to Rawlinson. 'It's all yours. As soon as you hear me give three bangs on the outside of the hatch, open up fast. By the time it's open you should have the first canoe right up behind it. If I blow one long blast on the whistle, you shut the hatch and clamp it, and it doesn't matter who's up top. You don't wait for anyone to get inside. That clear?'

'Yes, sir. All clear.'

Sub reported to the Captain that all was ready. The Major turned to his officers and said, 'Right. Get dressed.' The four of them went forward, collecting the sergeants on the way. Their packs were in the for'ard compartment with the canoes.

Shortly after nine o'clock, an unrecognizable Major returned to the wardroom. He was wearing an unusual sort of green battledress uniform, and all over him was strapped every sort of weapon from a knife to a Tommy-gun. His face and hands were blackened.

'We're all set, Hallet,' he told the Captain. The latter stared at him, then turned to Number One. 'Look out for me here, Number One. I'm going for'ard for a moment.'

In the for'ard Mess the Captain found seven other apparitions. He felt glad that he was not a guard on the beach: these quiet gentlemen who had sipped tea in the wardroom looked viciously efficient. He said,

'So long, you fellows. It's been nice having you. See you in a couple of days, and I can speak for all this ship's company when I say good luck. Au revoir, Major. Give 'em hell.' He shook the black hands, one by one, and he felt ridiculously emotional.

'Cheerio, old man,' said the Major. 'You've done a thundering good job for us. Day after tomorrow: two blue flashes, eh?'

'Two blue flashes,' agreed the Captain, and he turned on his heel and made his way back to the Control Room.

'Red lighting,' he ordered. 'Diving Stations in five minutes' time.'

CHAPTER SEVEN

'Stand by to surface.'

The Captain stared into the periscope as he gave the order and the report came back from the compartments. They had closed in towards the beach, as close as they could go submerged. Number One turned to the Captain.

'Ready to surface, sir.'

The Captain took a final look all round, then stepped back, and Featherstone sent the periscope down.

'Surface!'

Sub was standing by in the wardroom with Bird and three other seamen. As soon as the Captain and the Signalman had vanished up the ladder into the Conning Tower, he brought his party into the Control Room where they stood waiting for the order to go aloft.

'Slow ahead together,' came the order from the bridge, and the messenger sprang to the telegraphs. They were moving in.

'Control Room!'

'Control Room.'

'Casing party on the bridge.' Sub jumped on to the ladder and his party scrambled up behind him.

On the bridge, he caught his breath at the unusual sight. They were right up to the beach, a short, low-lying piece of land with the ground on either side rising sharply into cliffs. There was no moon, but they were so close that the silhouette of the land was quite clear, the high cliffs towering over the submarine. He wondered if anyone on those cliffs might be watching, waiting.

'All right Sub. Carry on.' Over the side of the bridge, finding the cut-away footholes by long practice without having to grope. As he hurried for'ard along the casing he grabbed a wheelspanner from Bird who was close behind him, jumped down the three steel steps on to the pressure-hull and banged three times on the hatch with the wheel-spanner. He heard the clatter inside as they took off the last clip: evidently the T.I. had lost no time, because almost immediately the big hatch swung open. Sub grabbed the block with the ropes running through it and hooked it quickly on an eyebolt on the casing outside the hatch. The bow of the first canoe rushed up towards him as the men down below heaved away on the tackle: he grabbed it, snatched off the spring-hook and dropped the gear back into the hatch. Bird and another man were already lowering the first canoe over the side: it slid rasping down the side of the casing and rode alongside. The Major and his sergeant were on the casing, climbing down over the side, and thirty seconds after the time that the hatch swung open the soldiers released the lines holding the canoe and the first one had gone. The second canoe was on the casing, and down below in the forward compartment they were snapping the spring-hook on to the bow of the third. Nobody had said a word.

The pitch-black night swallowed the tiny craft with their circling paddles: the sounds they made were inaudible at more than ten yards' range. The fourth and last canoe was gone: Bird threw all the lines and loose gear into the hatch, and he and his men jumped after it. Sub slammed it down and as he turned away to get back to the bridge he heard the men inside working at the clips.

The sea lay as flat as a slab of polished marble, the air warm and soft. The coastline rose black behind her as the submarine turned and headed slowly, silently, out into the Straits. The Captain said,

'All right, Sub, you go down. Tell Number One to go to Patrol Routine, and run all the fans. I'll stay up here. We'll dive in an hour.'

There was a feeling of anti-climax. The wardroom seemed almost deserted, with only the few submariners to share it. In the Petty Officer's Mess the Cox'n looked round the tiny space and murmured, 'Blimey – what'll we do with all this flippin' room?' Up forward, the seamen were putting their gear back in its place. All thoughts were with the soldiers, hoping for them and touching wood. They had made themselves many good friends in the past week, shown themselves as good messmates. On the bridge, the Captain stared at the coast, expecting at any moment to hear the sharp rattle of machine-guns or see the dazzling swoop of an alarm-rocket. But all was quiet, as quiet as the grave.

The men were at their Diving Stations, the fans stopped. From the voice-pipe came the order, 'Dive, dive, dive.' As the Captain shut the voice-pipe in the bridge and jumped into the hatch, Featherstone pulled out the levers that opened the vents, and the messenger shut the valve on the bottom of the voice-pipe.

Slowly, silently, the submarine sank on an even keel, no way on, just settling down towards the bottom. The Captain and Number One watched the depth-gauge, as Number One worked the order instrument and the internal tanks were gradually flooded to bring the submarine down to the bottom of the Straits.

'Another five feet, about.' She was still going down, very slowly, the needle crawling round the gauge. Then the slightest of bumps from for'ard, and she settled on the mud. Flood a little more in the for'ard trimming tank, the weight to act as an anchor. She was bottomed.

The Captain spoke quietly. 'We'll be staying here until midnight tomorrow night. Then we'll surface for two hours and run the fans, and dive again until the next night when we pick up the Army.

'Any man who makes a noise of any sort will be for it in a big way. If one of your stokers, Chief, drops a wheel-spanner in the Engine Room, I'll kick him to death. Any sound can give us away. There are to be no lights other than what's absolutely necessary, and no unnecessary movement. I want everyone off watch to sleep, all the time if they can. That won't be difficult, for some of you.' The Captain glanced at Chief again as he said it.

'Right, Number One. The Hands can go into four watches. Officers of the Watch as usual. Carry on.'

It is always quiet in a dived submarine at Patrol Routine. Now, under these circumstances, there was not even the low hum of the motors, nor any noise from the air-conditioning plant. Silence, complete silence, such as a lone mountaineer knows and few others in a noisy world have ever encountered, settled through the compartments. A coarse whisper in the Control Room raised a smile in the wardroom. The silence was deadening, suffocating, as the heat began to build up in the steel tube which, lying in tepid, shallow water, would be like an oven when the sun rose in the morning.

Number One shook Chief violently by the shoulder to wake him up. Chief looked up angrily from his sweat-damp bunk.

'Lie on your side, damn you. You've been snoring. I thought it was the klaxon.'

The Captain lay on his bunk, smiling to himself as he thought about his last leave and Bird, the Second Cox'n. On their last evening he and Chief had quite a few bottles left intact, and so they hired a small room on the ground floor of the hotel and invited a score of the *Seahound*'s sailors, who were spending their leave in the local rest-camp, to come up. It turned out to be a riotous evening, with much singing as the spirits sank in the bottles and rose in the men. The Manageress, a little woman who could easily have been a blood-relation of a hen, met Bird when he was on the way to the lavatory. Bird was singing at the top of his voice, and she told him to be quiet. He was in no mood to be treated in that manner by a person whom he considered to be a 'silly old geyser', and after a certain amount of Billingsgate repartee he gave chase, brandishing the gong-stick and uttering threats.

As they flashed through the small lounge, the Captain observed, 'She shows a remarkable turn of speed, for her age.'

Chief agreed. ' 'm. But I'd put my money on Bird, from the point of view of endurance.'

'Oh, dear,' said the Captain. 'I suppose I'd better do something. Shadwell – Parrot – go and catch Bird and put some sense into him.'

A few minutes later they brought him back, fed-up and depressed. 'Proper flippin' leave this is,' he complained.

Looking back, afterwards, on those two days spent lying on the bottom, none of them could produce very clear recollections.

It took in their minds the form of a pipe-dream: it was seen through a haze of heat, an opaque, heavy curtain of heat that hung over the eyes and dulled the ears, choked and stifled any coherent thought about how the time had been spent. There were blurred recollections of waking in a bunk that was a pool of sweat, taking over a watch in a silent Turkish Bath of irritation, depression and impatience. There were vague memories of meals that consisted always of corned beef, corned beef that was unrecognizable because it had melted into a greasy soup which was eaten with dry bread because the butter ran like water and could only have been poured on from a jug. There were memories of the Captain and the First Lieutenant forcing men to put salt in their drinking water to replace the salt that they were losing in sweat, and the taste of the warm salted water mingled with the blanket of heat, until you felt that you could scream, but no screaming would have made any difference.

In the After Mess, a very young stoker began to giggle to himself, and he went on giggling for over an hour in spite of his messmates' attempts to stop the horrible noise. After a time the Leading Stoker had a word with Stoker Johnson, who was a large, very powerful and kindly man, and Johnson stopped the giggling in the only possible way, a short, swift right-arm jab to the jaw that brought relief to everyone and was just in time to stop a few others giving way to the pressure in their brains.

In the middle of the night the nightmare was interrupted when they surfaced for two hours and ran the fans to clear the air. It was a relief, but the faces of the men as they stood open-mouthed gulping in the cool night air, noisily like pigs at a trough, bore expressions of weary apprehension, the faces of men whose torture would shortly be resumed, as resumed it was when at two in the morning the hatch crashed down and they sank to the bottom to do it all over again.

At eleven o'clock on the second night the Captain, wearing a strip of torn shirt round his head to keep the sweat out of his eyes, walked into the Control Room and said, 'Diving Stations.' To the men who heard it, the order meant only one thing: relief, fresh air, cool air. To the Captain it meant much more. It meant that within an hour he would know whether they'd failed or succeeded, whether the Major and his men were dead or alive. If the party failed to appear at midnight, or by one o'clock, which was the agreed time-limit, his orders were to leave the area. It would mean, if the soldiers were not there, that they were either killed or captured, and that meant that the enemy would have an idea that a submarine was at the bottom of the Straits. In those circumstances his duty was to save his ship, and nothing else. This was the zero hour.

Number One disturbed his thoughts. 'Ready to surface, sir.'

'Surface.' Water was pumped out of the trimming tanks, and after a few minutes they felt the submarine move. The needle jerked a little in the depth gauge, and began to circle slowly. At periscope depth the Captain ordered, 'Up periscope,' and carefully searched round. He stayed at the periscope for five minutes, while Number One battled with the trim and the submarine moved slowly ahead on one motor.

'Surface!' The word was music.

The Signalman stands in the centre of the bridge, behind the Captain and the Sub-Lieutenant. The Captain's glasses are motionless, fixed on the small strip of beach. Sub keeps an all-round lookout, continually resisting the temptation to stop his glasses on the shore and watch for the signal. Below, in the Control Room, Bird and his men wait under the hatch. Up for'ard, the T.I. and his torpedo-men sit in the empty Mess and wait.

Suddenly there's a gasp from the Captain.

'Signalman!' The Signalman jumps to his side, the blue lamp ready. The Captain speaks again: 'No – wait ... Yes, by God! on the left edge of the beach. Two blue flashes ... Give 'em two flashes, damn you!' The Signalman sights his lamp at the beach, presses the trigger twice. The Captain shouts down the voice-pipe.

'Tell the T.I. to stand by. Tell the First Lieutenant to be ready for any casualties. Slow ahead together. Casing party on the bridge.'

He straightens up, and says quietly to the Sub, 'Go on down. Don't open up until I give you the word.' A few minutes pass, and the Captain sees the first canoe, half-way between the shore and the submarine. He shouts over the front of the bridge, 'Stand by! Open up, Sub!'

Out of the night shoots the first canoe: it slides alongside, and they grab hold of it, lying on the casing. The men scramble out and Bird and Parrot lift the canoe out of the water and slide it into the hatch where hands are waiting to receive it. The Major climbs down after it, but the man with him is no sergeant. He is small, grey-haired, a civilian in a crumpled, off-white suit. They are too busy to wonder about it as the next canoe comes alongside: it contains Captain Bowers and his sergeant. The third canoe is manned by only one sergeant, the other cockpit empty. The last one holds young Montgomery and his sergeant.

All the canoes are inside. 'Down you go,' jerks out Sub, out of breath from the exercise: his men leap into the hatch, and he slams it shut and hurries aft along the casing to the bridge. He's wondering who the little civilian is, and where are Captain Selby and one sergeant. At the same time he's thinking 'We've done it!'

The Major shook hands warmly with the Captain. He looked just about at the end of his tether, and so did his men. They had been burnt raw by the sun and looked as though they had had no sleep in all the forty-eight hours.

'This,' said the Major, 'is Mr Jones.' The Captain shook hands with the little civilian.

Mr Jones, in spite of his dishevelled and careworn appearance, bore a certain dignity. It seemed possible to the Captain that he had another name and possibly even a uniform when he was elsewhere. The Major, at any rate, treated him with a comradely respect. They seemed to know each other well, and yet occasionally the Major took some trouble in stopping just short of the word 'Sir'.

'Where are the other two, Major?' asked the Captain. The Major smiled.

'Oh, don't worry about them.' The subject was closed.

After the soldiers and Mr Jones had eaten a large meal of corned beef, cold potatoes and mayonnaise sauce, followed by bread and cheese and coffee, the Captain pressed the buzzer for the table to be cleared. Then he reached into a locker and placed four tumblers on the table. He unlocked a cupboard and produced a new bottle of Scotch.

'It's all yours, gentlemen.' The Major asked him, 'Aren't you going to join us?'

'No, thanks. We don't at sea. Save up our thirsts until we get into Trinco.'

Presently the Major asked him whether he could give the sergeants a tot. Number One said, 'The Cox'n's looking after them, sir. Rum.'

'Oh,' said the Major. 'Well, here's to the *Seahound*. God bless you all.'

The diesels were taking them north, four hundred and twenty revolutions a minute up the Straits. They weren't sorry to be on the move.

They stood on the bridge, the Captain, the Major, Mr Jones and Number One who was the Officer of the Watch. The *Seahound* was out of the Straits and clear of the enemy, way out in the Indian Ocean.

The Landing Party were now fit again, well fed and rested, in boisterous spirits. Even Mr Jones's emaciated form had new life in it.

The aircraft, a Catalina, swept round in a big arc as it eased itself down to the water, then straightened up and touched down gently, taxied towards the submarine that lay stopped and waiting. The Captain shouted down: 'Send up the rest of the Army.'

The crew of the aircraft came out on the wings with cameras to take photographs of the submarine. The Major snarled:

'I'll have all those films exposed, in ten minutes' time.' Security, to the Major, was like air to a deep-sea diver.

The aircraft's crew floated a rubber dinghy down to the submarine on a long line. One at a time, Mr Jones first and the Major last, the party was hauled across. The canoes were left in *Seahound*.

The Major and the Captain exchanged salutes, and shook

127

hands. The farewells had all been said. They looked into each other's faces, and were genuinely sorry that they might not meet again.

The Captain noticed that as Mr Jones climbed up into the Catalina, he was greeted with a considerable number of salutes.

With the signal that had ordered *Seahound* to meet the Catalina had come the order for their recall, and as soon as the Army men were safely transferred to the big flying-boat the Captain turned his ship on to the homeward course. Over the broadcasting system he congratulated the ship's company on their conduct during the difficult time at the bottom of the Straits. 'I'm proud of you,' he said, and he meant it. They settled down to the passage routine, looking forward to the rest that lay ahead of them, the baths and the other small comforts that were always luxuries for the first few days in harbour. The Captain looked forward to a letter from Cynthia, Sub thought about where he'd go for his leave and decided on Colombo, and Number One thought about Mary-Ann. They were sitting in the wardroom, Chief on his bunk as usual and the Navigator on watch, when Number One dropped his bombshell.

'Sir,' he asked the Captain, 'what would you say if I asked permission to get married?'

'Good God! Are you serious?'

'Yes, I am.'

'Well I don't suppose it'd make the slightest difference what I said, would it?'

'Er – not really, sir. But I believe one has to ask.'

'I suppose she's white?'

The Petty Officer Telegraphist handed the Captain a cipher. 'Just received, sir.'

'Well, let's see what it's about. Here you are Chief, get moving.' Chief sat up, mumbling to himself about the lack of peace and quiet and some people having to do all the work. The Captain threw him a pencil and Number One shoved a signal-pad across the table. Chief began to thumb wearily through the book.

'God damn and blast!' he said, suddenly. Their recall was

128

cancelled. A Japanese cruiser had left Singapore, was believed to be trying to reach Rangoon to attack the Allied shipping that was concentrating there. All submarines were dispersed to cover every possible avenue of approach: *Seahound* was being sent to patrol off Port Blair, in the Andaman Islands.

Chief flung the pencil down on the table and said, 'Lot of bloody nonsense. The Japs wouldn't be such fools as to send a cruiser this far west.'

The Captain didn't agree.

'It's just the sort of thing they would do, Chief. They know they've had it, and we're closing in. So a quick suicide raid is very Jap-like. Sink a lot of ships and throw away a cruiser in the process.'

'Well,' said Chief, 'all that this is going to mean is three boring bloody days off those horrible little islands. We'll be back in Trinco three days later than we should have been, and we won't have seen a thing. If there is a cruiser, and not just a Flying Dutchman or a pink elephant, you can be quite sure it won't come anywhere near us.'

The Captain was not there to hear Chief's last speech. He was ordering a new course and an increase in speed. Chief heard the quickened tempo of the engines: scowling, he rushed aft to the Engine Room.

Sub went for'ard to the Petty Officers' Mess, to have a word with Chief Petty Officer Rawlinson.

'Want me, sir?' asked the T.I.

'D'you remember, T.I., saying a few days ago that there wouldn't ever be a target worth a torpedo?'

'That's right, sir. They don't need me in this ship. They need a flippin' artillery sergeant.'

'What would you say, T.I., if I told you that a Jap cruiser had left Singapore and might be coming this way?'

'Well, sir, begging your pardon, I'd say you was off your rocker.'

Nobody was very excited, and most of the men were fed-up to hear that their recall had been cancelled. Nobody was fool enough to think that anything as big as a cruiser would come their way: that sort of thing didn't happen. Anyway, they had had all the excitement they wanted in this patrol, and the idea of hanging around the Andamans in the hope of a bit more was not popular.

'Flippin' drudge, we are in this ship,' remarked Rogers as he clipped his toe-nails. 'Any flippin' job they 'ave, they say, "Oh, give it ter *Sea'ound*, she's the flippin' sucker roun' 'ere." I 'spect ole Fatty' (he referred to the Captain of the Submarine Flotilla) 'looks at his flippin' yeoman and says, "What's this? The *Sea-'ound* coming back to Trinco? Can't 'ave that – send her a flippin' signal and tell her to go and flip around the bleedin' Andamans for a bit." An' orf we go.'

'Well,' put in Shadwell, 'it'd be nice to sink a flippin' cruiser, wouldn't it?'

'Don't be barmy. There ain't no flippin' cruiser. They'll find it was all a flippin' great mistake. Some bastard had a drop too much and he got carried away, like. Gawd 'elp us – another flippin' cake-an'-arse party off the perishin' Andamans.'

'Me own opinion,' stated Hopkins, 'is that it ain't fair for us to go sinking cruisers out 'ere. We ought to leave 'em for the Yanks. We've had our share of cruisers an' suchlike, in the Med., and up north. It's only right to let the Yankies sink a couple, before the flippin' war ends.'

All over the Indian Ocean submarines were preparing to intercept the raider. *Setter* was heading for the Nicobar Islands, *Slayer* was putting on full speed to patrol off Penang, others were already in their allotted areas. A flotilla of destroyers was being rushed from Trincomali to Rangoon to protect the shipping in case the cruiser did break through.

Seahound would be off Port Blair when she dived at dawn on the next morning. It was off the Andamans that she had spent her first patrol when she arrived in the Far East. It had been a boring three weeks, with only one trawler sunk and a long fruitless search for the crew of a shot-down bomber. They couldn't imagine meeting anything worth sinking in that area, off the Andamans: it was always empty.

It was quiet and warm in the wardroom, while the Navigator kept the watch and they slept, most of them; only the Sub lay awake with his eyes shut letting his imagination run on the

130

subject of sinking cruisers. He saw it happen, heard the torpedoes exploding, several hits one after the other, and he said a prayer in his mind: 'God, let us meet the cruiser, and sink her.' He took it back: 'No, God, let us meet her, that's all.' It was up to you, the sinking part: if God lets you meet her, and you bungle it, you can't blame Him.

It always feels wonderful to have sunk a really good target: you're all so pleased with yourselves, and you know that when you get back to harbour they'll be waiting to show you that in their opinion you've done a good job. The way they do that is to line the ships with men, and cheer you into your berth: for a really big sinking, any merchant ships that may be there blow their sirens, the 'V' sign predominant, three short blasts and a long one, the little sign linked for all time with the greatest Englishman of the century.

It feels good to be cheered into harbour. To be cheered anywhere, in fact. The first time you ever had a cheer directed at yourself was when you were eight years old, and it was the village children that cheered you when you rode through the main street with the fox's blood on your cheeks – your first kill, and the ceremony of 'blooding': there was no reason for the children to have cheered, because it was something that had happened to you and not something that you had done, but it was an old custom, as English as roast beef, and it was dear to their hearts and so they cheered. The next time that you got a cheer was when you were twelve, and this time it was in Switzerland when you finished a test in a very fast *schluss* that took you through the arch of the finishing-post like a streak of light. You were covered in snow and there were icicles hanging in your hair because you'd fallen so many times, but you'd made up the time and won the badge with two stars on it, and you were only twelve so the people cheered.

Thinking of the cruiser he drifted into sleep, and there it was, the cruiser, making a terrific bow-wave of snow as it crossed the hillside, and Chief was sliding down on a toboggan with blood all over his face. It looked as though they were bound to collide, Chief and the cruiser, and Sub tried to shout, to warn him, but the words wouldn't come because his mouth was full of snow. The messenger was shaking him by the shoulder, saying, 'Sub-

Lieutenant, sir: five minutes to.' It was his turn to go on watch. The messenger, however, was used to shaking men for their watches, and he stood by until he knew that Sub was actually turning out and not going back to sleep again.

If the cruiser is coming this way, it means that she must have gone a long way round, maybe visiting the Nicobars first. That's quite possible, of course. But this is wishful-thinking, because you know, as you shove your feet into the rubber-soled shoes, that the chances of your meeting a cruiser are very slight indeed. It's like having a ticket in a sweepstake, and who ever wins a sweepstake except the other man?

The Navigator shows you the patrol-line on the chart, and the position which he has just fixed. Not trusting Navigators, you check his fix before you take over, because the submarine is close to the island and once you've taken over the watch the responsibility is all yours. He tells you the course, and you note that the telegraphs are at slow ahead together. 'O.K.' you say, and the Pilot goes to his bunk, fed-up because he'd been hoping that the cruiser would come along during his watch. Everyone likes to make the sighting.

'Up periscope.' No periscope watch will ever have been more efficient than the one you're going to keep during the next two hours. There's the island, steep and bright green: the sight of it recalls the atmosphere of the first patrol, when you'd just arrived in the East and everything was new and unusual. There's the entrance to the harbour of Port Blair, the entrance that the trawler came out of, the entrance that she limped back into, sinking and on fire. Behind the port the island rises to a conical hill which is so densely wooded that it looks as though it's made of trees, an enormous bouquet of emerald green against the deep blue of the sky. There is the watch-tower, a white box on stilts, from which the Jap sentry watches for a glimpse of a periscope. At the inshore end of the patrol-line, using the magnification in the periscope, you can see the sentry standing in his box, and you feel an urge to be on the surface so that you can turn him inside-out with a burst from the Oerlikon. You feel it as personally as that. Along the coastline you can remember the places from where the coast artillery fired at you as you fought the trawler; their shooting had not been at all bad, and the Captain had been forced to zigzag about while you directed the gun: it made it awkward, with the range and deflection changing between every few shots.

'Down periscope.' You fiddle with the trim for a minute, then turn again and signal with a movement of your hands for the periscope. It rushes up and you sweep all round with the air-search first, to make sure that while you search the horizon there will be no aircraft diving on the periscope. The sky is clear, and you sweep the horizon, first quickly to check that there is nothing in the immediate vicinity, then slowly, very slowly, so as not to miss the slightest sign of an enemy. And there, on the starboard beam as you head out from the island, there on the horizon in the south, in the direction in which the Nicobar Islands lie, you see a tiny smudge on the horizon. Smoke.

'Captain in the Control Room.' He's there so fast that you only have time to dip the periscope: it comes up again into his hands. As he looks, the men whose eyes are fixed anxiously on his face see a slow smile twist his lips. They have seen that look before.

'Diving Stations!' As Number One tumbles out of his bunk, he says, 'My God – must be the cruiser!'

'Don't be a silly flipper,' answers Chief. He's never at his best when he's woken abruptly. 'Cruiser be damned.'

At Diving Stations, the submarine turns and heads towards the smoke. Number One is thinking, after he's been told that it's smoke, that it'll turn out to be either a cloud or a mirage. But the Captain, watching through the periscope, knows better. It's smoke, and the smoke of a big ship.

'Oh, hell. She's escorted, by the looks of it.' He's seen a second, a smaller smudge. Ten minutes pass slowly.

'I can see her, now. Stand by all tubes.' The order is passed for'ard, to the astonished T.I.

'Yes, it's a cruiser. Two destroyers. Stand by to start the attack.' The Navigator is ready with a stop-watch in his hand.

'Start the attack. Bearing – that! Range – that! I'm fifteen on her starboard bow.'

Sub with his calculating machine, and the Navigator with his

133

track-chart, soon have a picture of the cruiser's movements. This is the Attack Team in action, the result of many practices on dummy targets in the depot-ship's 'Attack Teacher', and of many dummy attacks during the 'work up' period before they left Scotland. Each man knows that one slip, one inaccuracy on his part, could produce a wrong answer that would leave the cruiser afloat. Only the Captain sees anything but the figures and the track lines on the plotting diagram.

'How long has the attack been going?'

'Eleven minutes, sir.' In his mind Sub sees the cruiser as the Captain passes on the picture in figures. The enemy course and speed have been calculated, checked and rechecked each time a new range and bearing is taken, and added to the picture on the track chart.

'Starboard twenty.' The submarine turns on to her firing course, a course worked out in relation to the enemy's course so that the torpedoes will approach her at an angle of ninety degrees, on her beam.

'Course two-two-five, sir.'

'Very good. Stand by!'

The order is flashed forward to the men at the tubes.

'Fire one!' Thud and shudder, a hiss and the rising pressure.

'Fire two!'

'Fire three!' Half the salvo is on its way. Saunders says:

'Torpedoes running, sir.'

'Fire four!' God, let them hit!

'Fire five!'

'Fire six! – Flood "Q", a hundred and fifty feet, full ahead together, port twenty-five!'

Now to get out of it: the torpedoes are on their way, and whether they hit or miss is out of anyone's hands. But the destroyers will be active in a minute.

'Shut off for depth-charging.' The words are hardly spoken and repeated by the man at the telephone when the submarine is rocked by the explosion of the first torpedo striking home into the cruiser, then another and yet a third. Three hits: a certain kill. In the Engine Room, Chief grins at the Stokers.

'Now we're for it, lads.'

*

Before the submarine was shut off and the bulkhead doors shut, Sub went forward to be with the T.I. and the torpedomen. The Officers' stations for depth-charging were: Sub forward, the Navigator in the Accommodation Space, the Captain and Number One in the Control Room. Each compartment was sealed off by its water-tight doors.

Sub grinned at the T.I. 'Well, Rawlinson, we sank the bastard. Three hits – not bad, eh?'

'I still can't believe it, sir. We expecting trouble, now?'

'Expect so. There are two destroyers up there.' As he spoke, they heard one of the destroyers race across overhead. Her propellers churning the water made a noise like an express train going past. The T.I. looked round at his men.

'Now lads,' he said, 'there'll be some dirt flying in a moment. It always sounds worse than it is.'

'That's all right, Nursey,' answered Shadwell. 'We've all 'eard it before. Bring on the flippin' dancing-girls.'

No charges had been dropped, that time, but a moment later they heard the screws again. They seemed to pass on the port side and fade away ahead. Just before the sound faded, the first pattern of charges went off, a tearing crash that was too close, a sort of *zonk* effect as the blast bounced off the hull.

'That ain't no flippin' good,' remarked a torpedoman. ''Ave to do better 'n that, old chums.'

'Don't call those buggers chums, or I'll do yer,' muttered Shadwell. The second destroyer made her run, evidently across the stern. The explosions seemed to be astern, anyway, but closer than the first lot. The submarine was shaken, and cork chips rained down from the paint overhead.

'Gettin' warmer,' said Parrot.

'They're not a patch on the Gerries, or the Wops, are they, sir?' The T.I. was speculating on the relative efficiency of the Axis powers. 'Why, I remember once in the Med., off Sicily, we —'

That lot was bad. Sub was thrown across the compartment, landed in a heap with the T.I. and Parrot. The submarine had been rolled over and her stern thrown up by the exploding charges. It wouldn't have to be much nearer than that. The telephone buzzed, and Sub answered it. It was the Control

Room, a message from the Captain: 'Report the situation for'ard.' 'Everything's in order,' said Sub. He put the receiver back and grabbed hold of a stanchion as another pattern deafened them, shaking the submarine as a terrier shakes a rat.

In the Control Room, Number One fought with the trim, bringing the submarine out of a dive at two hundred and seventy feet.

'Two hundred feet,' ordered the Captain. 'Port thirty, full ahead together.' Twisting and turning, trying all the tricks, yet the enemy seemed not to be easily fooled. Another pattern exploded, but this time they hardly felt it.

'Rotten shot,' said the Captain. 'These Japs are no good.'

The Cox'n muttered: 'I don't think my Mum would like me to be 'ere.'

The next pattern was a long time coming, a pause of about five minutes, while Saunders reported that one of the destroyers had stopped and that the other was going away. Then he reported, 'Bearing drawing left, sir.'

'Very good.' The Captain acknowledged the report.

'Coming towards, sir. She's turned round.'

'Very good.' The Captain ordered an alteration of course: 'Starboard fifteen.'

The other destroyer, stopped, was in contact. They could hear the *pings*, like a mouse squeaking on the hull.

'Hundred and fifty feet, Number One.'

'Hundred and fifty feet, sir.' The needle was only just steady at the new depth when they heard the destroyer passing close again.

'Starboard twenty.' The helmsman swung his wheel over, his face as expressionless as the bulkhead door. Charges were on their way down, by now. A few seconds passed, and they seemed to explode under their feet, throwing the submarine up like a cork. Men were flung about, those who had unwisely not been holding on to anything. Cork chips spattered on them, and the lights went out. Someone cursed: the emergency lighting glowed feebly, throwing deep shadows in the compartment. At ninety feet, Number One got the angle under control, and they began to get down again. The lights came on.

'Report from the Motor Room,' snapped the Captain. He was

bleeding from a cut on his forehead, and he dabbed at it with a handkerchief.

'All correct, sir. The switch threw off.'

'A hundred and fifty feet!'

'Hundred and fifty, sir.'

In the Engine Room, Chief and the Stoker Petty Officer sat on the steel step and swapped stories with the stokers. Stoker Johnson was just finishing one.

' "Blimey",' she said, ' "so that's what it's for!" '

They all laughed, although Chief didn't think it was particularly funny. He had heard lots of dirty stories, but he rarely thought any of them worth telling, and he thought that most were better not told at all. He could never remember the funny ones, the ones he wanted to remember. Only the stupid, sordid ones. He turned to the Stoker P.O.

'Have you heard the one,' he asked, 'about the errand boy?'

'No,' answered the Petty Officer, 'I don't think so, sir.' He listened to it, right through to the end, through a pattern of depth-charges that sent the submarine down to three hundred and fifty feet, and at the end he joined in the general laughter. But he didn't see anything funny in it, either; and in any case he had, actually, heard it before.

The hunt went on, and pattern after pattern exploded savagely round the submarine, which twisted and turned like an eel, twisted and turned in three dimensions as she altered depth sometimes deliberately and sometimes because the charges sent her temporarily out of control. In the for'ard Mess they had grown used to it, powerless to do anything but hang on and wait as the explosions came at more or less regular intervals and they felt the lift and tilt of the deck under their feet. The deck was carpeted in the cream-coloured chips of cork and paint. Shadwell stared at it gloomily.

'We'll 'ave this flippin' lot to clean up, I suppose, soon as them bastards get sick of droppin' muck on us.' As he spoke a pattern exploded, a harsh, ringing crash. Sub, his eyes on the deckhead, could almost imagine that he saw the plates bulging inwards under the impact.

Chief Petty Officer Rawlinson's hands, hidden in the pockets of his shorts, were clenched into fists. An experienced submariner, the survivor of dozens of such attacks, he knew that *Seahound* would not stand much more of this hammering. If the enemy held the contact, it would only be a matter of time. Ten minutes? ... Half-an-hour? Nobody could tell when the last pattern would do its work. He looked up, and met the Sub-Lieutenant's eyes: through the mask that each of them had assumed, each could see that the other was under no delusions as to how things were going. Shadwell knew, too: he sat on the deck with his arms round his knees, singing softly, under his breath, a song about a lady of easy virtue.

Five minutes had passed since the last charges. Sub studied his watch, not letting himself give way to any premature hopes of escape. The T.I., seeing his action, pursed his lips and strained his ears for the sound of returning propellers. But all seemed quiet, still.

Ten minutes had passed. They looked at each other, and now in Rawlinson's seasoned face was the dawn of relief. Five minutes later, when for a quarter of an hour the submarine had seemed to be steady and keeping an even depth while no explosions shattered the tense underwater silence, Sub looked round and grinned.

'Looks as though they've lost us, T.I.'

'Shouldn't be surprised, sir.' Rawlinson was cleaning his nails with a small screwdriver.

As soon as *Seahound* surfaced that evening, the Petty Officer Telegraphist was busy tapping out a signal which Chief and Number One had spent the afternoon putting into cipher. When they had done it they gave it to the Captain to decipher, as a check, and they felt quite pleased with themselves when it came out into the original message again. The message announced the sinking with torpedoes of a Japanese cruiser of the *Yashima* class, the time and position of the sinking and the fact that the escort of two destroyers were believed to have left the vicinity of the Andamans at 1300 hours on a course approximately North-East by East. It added that *Seahound* had suffered no damage.

The telegraphist was still tapping when the Captain joined

the others in the wardroom. There wasn't much to say: the success was too big, too obvious, for comment. The Captain addressed the First Lieutenant:

'Number One – were there any breakages?'

'One or two, sir. Nothing very serious.'

'The Cox'n's Store – was a rum-jar broken, by any chance?'

Number One smiled an odd smile. 'There could easily have been, sir.' The Captain pressed the buzzer for a messenger.

'Sir?'

'Tell the Cox'n I want to see him.'

Chief Petty Officer Smith heaved happily into sight. 'See me, sir?'

'Cox'n – I believe a jar of rum was smashed during the fun and games this morning.'

'No, sir – I mean, yes, I believe one was, sir.'

'Very good, Cox'n. I'll write it off. And now – splice the mainbrace.'

'Aye aye, sir.' It meant a double issue of rum for all hands. including officers, rum that on paper did not exist, since the jar had been smashed during the depth-charging and its contents were now, officially, mingled with a certain amount of dirty water in the bilges.

These things had to be seen to in an official manner.

Supper was cleared away when the dots and dashes became audible from the wireless office, where the telegraphist on watch was receiving a signal. Chief was in such an unusual frame of mind that he started quite happily to gather his books together, and set to work humming to himself.

It was a signal acknowledging their last one, a signal of very hearty congratulations. The Captain read it out to the Ship's Company, over the broadcasting system. It had not been unexpected.

They realized afterwards how it was that they'd been lucky enough to get away with it. The Japanese squadron had sailed in a hurry, on last-minute orders. The two destroyers had only a few depth-charges on board, and they only had time before they sailed to get another truck-load each. This was discovered a week later, after the destroyers had been sunk by British destroyers and some prisoners were interrogated.

All the same, the score-board in the wireless office, where the Telegraphists sat during the depth-charging and made a cross for each explosion, showed a hundred and nineteen crosses.

Sub was dreaming about Sheila, Sheila and he in a canoe, and just at the moment, the embarrassing moment, that he was about to kiss her and she turned into Major Worth, he found himself awake on his bunk with a smell of fried breakfast and coffee in the air. Chief, who had shaken him out of his dream, was sitting there grinning at him.

'Look,' asked the Sub. 'What's going on?'

The Captain said: 'Many Happy Returns, Sub.' Chief said the same thing. Number One shook his hand and said, 'Congratulations, Sub.'

He'd forgotten all about it. It was his 21st birthday. Twenty-one: he'd been fighting in the war at sea for four years.

Chief handed him something wrapped up in a lot of brown paper and string. Sub took a dirty knife from somebody's used plate, and cut the string: he unwrapped the paper and found a huge key.

'Key of the door,' explained Chief. 'Featherstone filed it up last night.'

During his off-watch period, the E.R.A. had filed this outsize key from a lump of metal.

'Chef was busy too, last night.' Number One spoke. 'Made you a birthday cake. He says he's never baked a cake before, and he's worried about how it'll turn out.'

These were the gifts that counted; they were the emblems of friendship and affection of men who gave neither lightly.

'How does it feel to be twenty-one, Sub?'

'All I feel at the moment is hungry. Wilkins!' – They all started, and as he shouted the name the memory hit him in the pit of his stomach and his head swam with the way it hurt, and the fool he felt was plain in his face.

'I'm sorry. I'm damned sorry.' He thought: well, twenty-one isn't old enough, it seems. I'll have to be forty before I stop making frightful, unforgivable mistakes like that. With the one shout he had wrenched savagely at the new scar on a fresh, painful wound, and he had seen the quick, shocked pain in three faces. Now, in his mind, he saw the way Wilkins drooped and slumped as his lungs came out through his sides and the blood, the ribs and his grey broken face. Dear God, forgive ...

'Sub.'

'Sir.'

'Your breakfast is getting cold. And don't be a damn fool. Any of us could have done that.'

Yes, any of them could have, the habit of over a year of breakfasts combining with the sleepy brain. Any of them. The trouble was, it had been he. He thought to himself: it always is.

After the strain of watch-keeping in enemy waters, the watches on the surface on the way home across the Indian Ocean were a welcome relaxation. Clad only in a pair of shorts under the blazing sun the men recovered their tan, drank in fresh air and looked forward to the spell in harbour. They took things easily, and with the knowledge of the success behind them and the welcome ahead they were happy days.

Sub came off watch at noon, relieved by Number One while the Navigator took a noon sight of the sun. In this weather, taking a sight was simple: it was when the weather was really bad that the process became almost impossible, when as soon as the sextant reached the bridge, wrapped in a towel, a green wave hurled itself into the bridge and the wet sextant was useless. The terrific motion of the submarine was no help, either.

Sub had stepped off the ladder in the Control Room and turned round to make his way into the wardroom when Chief Petty Officer Rawlinson stopped him.

'Torpedo Officer, sir. There's a buzz that it's your twenty-first birthday today. That right, sir?'

'It is, T.I.' Sub's hand was grasped in the other man's, pumped vigorously up and down.

'All the best, sir. Could you spare a moment? – We'd like you to come for'ard, for a moment.'

They walked for'ard together, to the Petty Officers' Mess. The Cox'n and the Stoker Petty Officer greeted him warmly, and, after pulling the curtain across the entrance to the Mess, the Cox'n handed him a glass with an inch of dark brown rum in the bottom of it.

'Thanks, Cox'n.' Sub threw it down in one gulp, as a proper sailor should, and they watched with approval in their eyes. He shook hands with them all, hoping that the burn in his throat wouldn't make his eyes water and let him down in front of these men whose assessment of a man was valuable. As he left the little Mess, Shadwell was standing outside, waiting for him.

'Torpedo Officer, sir – would you come for'ard for a minute, please?'

Oh, my God. The Sub blinked. 'Certainly, Shadwell. What is it?' He pretended he didn't know what it was all about.

About a dozen sailors were waiting for him in the for'ard Mess. Bird handed him a glass of rum, and Rogers said, 'Dahn the 'atch, sir.' They watched him closely as he threw the rum back into his throat.

'Thank you, gentlemen. The best twenty-first I ever had.' They laughed, liking him. Rogers muttered, under his breath, 'Proper toff, young Subby.' Sub went aft to his lunch. The rum was warm in his stomach. What was it they called rum? – Nelson's Blood. No wonder Nelson was a ball of fire, with this stuff in his veins.

After lunch, Sub lay on his bunk, and he saw a picture of Sussex and the party that there would have been if he'd been at home. He could see all the faces that would have been round the table that evening, and he knew that he and those faces would never really know each other again. That had been the centre, the focal point of his life: now Sussex was only the background, something soft to think about.

These men were the friends he wanted, and this was the life he wanted to lead. That was why he knew that the future was going to be no good for him: he didn't want it. His young world was tottering on the precipice of peace.

CHAPTER EIGHT

With the coast of Ceylon in sight, all hands were turned-to to make *Seahound* look her best. This was to be their hour, probably *Seahound*'s last and greatest performance. Not the smallest piece of brass was left unpolished: by the time they were in the Bay, when Sub and the casing party came up, they felt as though they shouldn't walk on the bridge or touch any part of it. The Gunlayer gave his beloved gun an admiring glance as he passed it.

'All right, sir?'

'Not at all bad, Layer.' No submarine gun had ever looked better. Nobody would have thought that this submarine had been on patrol, and nobody would ever have dreamt that she had had such a rough handling. It was a strange thing, but understandable to a war-time flotilla, that a submarine arriving from her home port after a peaceful voyage could look weathered and battered, while the same submarine returning from a hard patrol could look like a showpiece for Navy Week.

Still out in the bay, they came in sight of the Depot Ship, and from her tall bridge a lamp flashed, a signal demanding that the submarine identify herself. The Signalman looked proud as he sent *Seahound*'s signal letter and number flashing across in answer. On the casing, Sub's party had the gear ready for going alongside, and now the men were lined up fore-and-aft, their white uniforms gleaming cleanly in the evening sun.

Over the submarine's bridge flew the Jolly Roger, their personal flag. Above and just to the left of the grinning skull was a new red bar that stood for the cruiser, and in the centre at the bottom was a white dagger, the sign of a Special Operation. Everything that they had done or destroyed was there on the flag, the record of their victories.

As *Seahound* swung into the gap in the boom defences, a shrill V-sign hooted from the siren of the little boom-vessel. On her grimy bridge stood an officer and three ratings, shouting and waving their caps. The Captain gave them a friendly wave as the submarine swept through and past: ahead lay the Depot Ship, her decks lined thickly with sailors. *Seahound* crossed the stern of the big ship, and the two exchanged salutes, the thin pipe and the lordly bugle-call in answer. As the last note of the bugle fell silvery across the harbour, a thousand men began to cheer, a barrage of applause, their caps raised high, a sea of white over the massed brown faces.

This welcome, this salute from a ship so big to one so small, from so many men to so few, this was the highest praise that a submariner could ever know. Nothing could ever, so long as they lived, put such a thrill of pride into their slightly hardened hearts: for here submariners were being saluted by submariners, and who could know better than submariners when such a salute was deserved, who know better than submariners how much it meant?

Slowing, the submarine slid alongside. Heaving lines flew high to fall across the casing: rapidly they were hauled over, dragging the heavier ropes. A moment later Number One shouted over the front of the bridge. 'Heave in for'ard!' And as he shouted he thought to himself that if all his life had been spent to accomplish the last ten minutes, it would have been worth living.

Chief, at the back of the bridge, had no orders to give. It was just as well. He would hardly have trusted himself to speak.

The wardroom was crowded. It was a party, and the Seahounds were not buying any of the drinks. The flotilla had a cruiser to its credit, and it was to *Seahound* that the flotilla owed it.

They had bathed, read their letters, drunk some gin and read the letters again. The Captain, leaning on the bar with one foot on the brass rail, was thinking about his own letters, when, glancing round, he saw Chief, a happy Chief who smiled down into his glass before he drank.

'Plenty of mail, Chief?'

'Plenty. One letter.'

'I'm sorry.' He knew that Chief's home affairs were wrong.

144

The Engineer had never spoken of it, never hinted at it, but in a submarine these things became plain. Particularly when two men knew each other as these did.

'It's all right. It really is. One letter, Arthur. Pam's joined the Wrens again: she's trying to get out here. Damn it, it's true! I'm not dreaming, am I?'

'You're not dreaming, Chief. I'm so damned glad. It's the best thing I've heard for months.'

'You know, I feel more engaged than married. Like looking forward to a honeymoon. Everything seems to have happened at once.'

'I think this calls for a gin.' The Captain called, and the gin came, and while they were drinking it Number One fought his way over to their end of the bar. He swayed slowly to and fro between the Captain and Chief.

'Been on the blower, sir.'

'Glad to hear it. Have a gin.'

'Thank you, sir. You did give me permission to get spliced, didn't you, sir?'

'Yes. Why – you're not going to, are you?'

'Yes, sir. Just asked her.'

There they were, thought the Captain, all of them, back again. Himself: well, he could see to that. Chief: married, and happy for the first time in two years. A solid, reliable man, old Chiefy. Work himself to death on the quiet, and still the same old grouse, the same steady, quiet influence in the ship, the same quiet control of his department. And Number One: always in the right place doing the right thing at the right time, never expecting any thanks for it. Both of these men, thought the Captain, deserved to be happy all day. Looking over his shoulder, he saw the Sub standing in a group of his young friends. There was the odd one: for his age, an enigma. Why should one so young be only happy on patrol, in action or with the prospect of it? Why should anyone feel like that? It paid dividends, though: the Captain knew that whenever they sailed, the weapons would be in tip-top condition, and on patrol he had noticed that the Sub seemed to regard every shell that missed as a personal failure. But the mainspring, the thing that made the youngster tick, was never in sight.

There they were, the team, the first eleven: four very different people blended into a unit which, placed at the head of a ship's company as good as *Seahound*'s, produced the answers.

'You're very quiet, sir.'

''m. Well, Chief, you're not the only one that gets letters, you know.'

The doctor, twiddling the knob of the loudspeaker, yelled for silence, and got it. The man in London came through loudly and clearly:

'An Admiralty communiqué issued an hour ago announces that the Japanese heavy cruiser *Yashima* has been torpedoed and sunk in the Indian Ocean by His Majesty's Submarine *Seahound*. The *Seahound* is commanded by Lieutenant-Commander Arthur Hallet, D.S.O., D.S.C., Royal Navy. The communiqué adds that the submarine underwent a severe depth-charge attack immediately after the sinking, but that no damage or casualties were sustained. The submarine has now returned to her base.

'Usually reliable sources in Washington have indicated the possibility of talks, in the not too distant future, to investigate opportunities for . . .' The doctor switched it off.

'Fame at last,' murmured the Captain. 'Steward: drinks all round, please.'

Tiny, after an hour in the bar, had engaged the Padre in a theological discussion. Interest in such matters was one of the stages which he passed through during any celebration: from God, he usually went on to ghosts. The Padre was accustomed to this routine, and did his best to humour the big man. Offering Tiny a cigarette from his tin, he argued, gently:

'But my dear old Tiny, if God did not forgive, Heaven would be empty!'

'How do you know it isn't?' Tiny smiled craftily.

'Well, one can —'

'You've never been there, have you?'

'Really, Tiny, if you're going to argue at all —'

'And if you drink any more of that stuff,' muttered Tiny,

darkly, 'you won't ever go there. You'll come along with the rest of us.'

The Sub goggled at his First Lieutenant.

'You don't mean it?'

'What in hell's the matter with you all? What's so funny about me getting engaged?'

'Nothing at all. Congratulations, and all that sort of thing.'

Tiny told him, 'We thought you were married already, to the jolly old White Ensign.' Sub laughed.

'When the Padre asks if there's any reason why this couple should not be joined together in Holy Matrimony, I'll jump up at the back of the church waving a White Ensign and shouting "Bigamy! Bigamy!"'

'That's enough from you, Sub. Go and fetch the bottle.' He muttered to Tiny, 'Damn fine reception a chap gets when he announces his engagement.' Tiny slapped him on the shoulder.

'The thing is, old boy, nobody believes you. They think it's the gin. But never mind, I'll believe you ... how many have you had tonight?'

Number One spent the next night in the submarine. One Officer was Duty each night, and had to sleep in the submarine instead of in his cabin in the Depot Ship. One third of the ship's company formed the Duty Watch and also slept on board.

At nine o'clock he did Rounds, walking through the boat from one end to the other, checking that all was safe and properly squared off. Rounds ended back in the Control Room, and Number One dismissed the Duty Petty Officer. The hands relaxed, returned to their letter-writing and other pastimes. Number One dropped into a chair in the Wardroom and reached out for a pile of letters that awaited censoring.

Censoring was a bore. He hated reading other peoples' letters, but it had to be done, and he had acquired the art of glancing rapidly down the page without taking in any of the private contents, only his eye catching any place-names, dates or words

147

like 'patrol'. He finished the last letter with a sigh of relief, stuck down the flap, stamped it 'Passed by Censor'. Then he put the pile of letters into the postbox outside the wardroom.

The system of having one night in three compulsorily on board was a good one in some ways, thought Number One, as he brought a heap of paperwork out of his drawer. It meant that this rubbish got dealt with instead of being put off from day to day and eventually causing trouble. Nobody liked paperwork, but everyone had to put up with it, everyone from the Captain of the Flotilla to the Cox'n of a submarine. But a good Depot Ship, like this one, could do a lot towards keeping it down to a minimum.

Amongst other things, the First Lieutenant had to keep the men's personal records up to date. Thumbing through a pile of them, he looked at the space in which each man's private occupation was noted. The Gunlayer was a market gardener, the Gun Trainer a brewery hand. Rogers had been a milkman, while Parrot had described himself as a grave-digger. Number One, as he looked through the papers, felt a slight envy of these men who had a second trade, while he had only one.

He stood up, switched on the loudspeaker over his head: it was time for the programme known as 'Forces Favourites'. A woman's voice announced a number for Alf, Pete and Stooge, who had been waiting to hear it for a long time and were looking forward to getting home to their families in Croydon. This record had also been asked for by the Bats Brigade of Number Six Mess, H.M.S. *Tapeworm*. The disc screamed into its millionth reproduction: of course, it had to be her, the Sweetheart of the Forces. He reached up, switched it off.

Before he turned in, at about eleven o'clock, Jimmy walked for'ard and climbed up through the hatchway into the cool, clear air. It was very quiet. *Seahound* lay with three other submarines of her own class: the one outside her had only that day returned from patrol. The four sister-ships rubbed sides, as though taking pleasure in each other's company, and there was about them even here an air of purpose as though they knew that they were only resting before new battles. The oily water lapped softly on their bulging saddle-tanks, and the submarines moved very slightly while the hemp ropes creaked as they strained under the changing weight.

"'night, Hodges.' The sentry saluted.

'G'night, sir.' Number One slipped quietly down the ladder, edged round a heavily-weighted hammock and went aft to turn in and to dream of Mary-Ann.

They lay spreadeagled, naked on the soft, warm sand, only blue sky in sight except, if you bent your head back, for the line of palms that fringed the beach. This was a wonderful place for bathing, Sweat Bay: the rest of the Fleet, the surface ships which were berthed in the other part of the harbour, used the crowded beaches to the north. Here the party of submariners was as often as not the only group on the beach.

Jimmy raised himself on his elbows.

'Come on, Tiny, you mass of blubber. Come and swim some of it off.'

'Quiet, Skinny. You're jealous of my manly body.'

Jimmy interrupted him, sitting up quickly and staring out to sea.

'What the hell?'

'Uh?' Sub sat up, looked the same way. Landing Ships.

'What are they?'

'Landing Ships.'

'Landing Ships?' Even Tiny sat up. 'What are they doing here?' Tiny always asked questions like that.

'Anchoring.' They were, too. The men on the beach heard the roar of the cables running out as they watched the fleet of queer-looking vessels: they hadn't known that there were any of these in the Indian Ocean.

'There are rather a lot of them,' observed Tiny. 'Reminds me of the gulf of Suez, a month or two before we went into Sicily.'

The ships were lowering their Assault Craft to circle around, more and more joining those already in the water. The sea was soon dotted with hundreds of the smaller craft. Gradually a certain order grew out of the mass: they were forming long queues alongside their parent ships, embarking men.

Tiny murmured, horrified, 'I hope they aren't all coming here!'

But they were: a wide arc of Assault Craft, a long unbroken line, was moving towards the beach. Soon it was possible to see the men in them. The line swept into the surf, anchors plumbed down from the sterns of the craft and their bows touched along the whole length of the beach. What looked and sounded like a crazy Army poured out over the sand, discarding shirts and trousers: white skin straight from England, not yet browned by the sun. An invasion fleet, or part of one, had evidently just arrived from its home ports.

Tiny gazed dismally at the crowded beach, and groaned.

'It's like Margate,' he commented. 'On a blasted Bank Holiday.'

Number One said, 'Looks more like an Invasion, to me. Coming to swim, Sub?'

As they walked down to the water, Number One muttered, 'Sub, I'm just beginning to get an idea of what we were doing down in the Straits with those soldiers.'

'Oh?'

'For Christ's sake, man: look!' Number One pointed at the mass of Landing Craft, the horde of men.

'A new D-Day, Sub. D-Day in Malaya. That's my guess.'

Perhaps, thought the Sub. Perhaps he's right. There was in these days a bigger thought that he had, a thought that had started when he heard a remark of Chief's, in the bar, on the night they returned from the last patrol. Chief had said to the Captain, 'Too many things are right tonight. Too many things, all at once. This sort of time doesn't come twice.'

Sub had bitten on to that thought. He thought that Chief was right. They had all been looking forward to Victory Day, VJ. They had discussed ways of celebrating it. Sub remembered a young Army man, a Lieutenant in the Tank Corps: they had been friends on the troopship, and when the Army units landed first at Suez and the Navy men leant on the rail to watch them go as they waited their own turn to land, someone had said to him, 'John, I don't think we'll see that soldier again.'

The soldier's tank had been blown up a few weeks later. Sub thought that perhaps the Seahounds had already seen their VJ Day: nobody would see a better one. But as he ran into the shallow warm water, he thought: I imagine too much; I think a lot of damn nonsense.

On the upper deck of the Depot Ship, all hands were fallen in for Sunday Divisions. The crew of each submarine was fallen in separately: in another place were the Spare Crew, and on the quarter-deck were the Depot Ship's own men. Orders rang out clearly over the harbour as the platoons were called to attention, inspected and stood at ease.

The Captain stopped opposite Able Seaman Rogers.

'Get a haircut, Rogers, and don't turn up for Divisions looking like that again.'

The Captain of the Flotilla walked round with his Staff, inspecting each platoon in turn. As he turned away from the last man in *Seahound*'s rear rank, he said to the Captain,

'Your men look fit, Hallet. Some of 'em could do with a haircut, though, eh?'

'Yes, sir.'

'Oh, Hallet: join me in my cabin, after Church.'

'Aye aye, sir.' The great man passed on to inspect another submarine's crew. The Captain snapped,

'Number One!'

'Sir?'

'See that those men have their hair cut before Rounds tonight.'

'Aye aye, sir.' Parrot, the submarine's unofficial barber, grinned to himself in the rear rank. It was an ill wind, he thought, that blew nothing in nobody's way.

'Seahound Ship's Company – right turn! Quick march!' They marched down on to the well-deck, which had been rigged under canvas for the church service. The Padre stood ready on a small dais: a table in front of him, covered with a Union Jack, was the altar. He had a little chapel, down below, but it was by no means big enough for all the men now ranged before him on benches across the wide deck.

'O Eternal Lord God, who alone spreadest out the heavens, and rulest the raging of the sea: who hast compassed the waters with bounds until day and night come to an end: Be pleased to receive into thy almighty and most gracious protection the persons of us thy servants, and the Fleet in which we serve. Preserve us from the dangers of the sea, and from the violence of the enemy: that we may be a safeguard unto our most gracious Sovereign Lord, King George, and his Dominions, and a security for such as pass on the seas upon their lawful occasions: that the inhabitants of our Island may in peace and quietness serve thee our God: and that we may return in safety to enjoy the blessings of the land, with the fruits of our labours, and with a thankful remembrance of thy mercies to praise and glorify thy Holy Name: through Jesus Christ our Lord.'

A low growl of 'Amen' rose from the ranks of sailors, and Arthur Hallet found in his mind the words of another prayer which, not long ago, it had been his duty to read to his men:

'Forasmuch as it hath pleased Almighty God of His great mercy to take unto Himself the soul of our dear brother here departed, we therefore commit his body to the sea...'

Over each peaceful ship in the harbour, a Church Pendant hung motionless in the still, hot air. The sea lay flat, blank-faced, hiding its million secrets.

Arthur Hallet knocked on the door of the Cuddy, heard the loud 'Come in!', placed his cap under his left arm and turned the door handle with his right hand.

'Gin or sherry, Hallet?'

'Gin, thank you, sir.' The Staff Officer, Operations, was there with Captain Meadows.

''Morning, Arthur.'

'Hello, Stinky.' He used the nickname under his breath. If Captain Meadows had discovered that his S.O.O. was commonly known as Stinky, that officer would never have heard the end of it. As things were, he had very little peace. Meadows was a big, florid man: he looked the conventional country squire, but that part had been allotted many years ago to his elder brother. He was a popular Captain (Submarines), as popular with the sailors as with their officers: his loud voice, powerful physique and even stronger language had endeared him to them all. Over and above that, he had a wide and accurate knowledge of his job, and a shrewd insight into the makings of a man. For a stranger it took a little time to learn these truths, since his bluff, sailor-like appearance and address gave a first impression of a man who was a bit of an old fool. Meadows was no man's fool.

'Plymouth, Hallet,' he observed, pointing to the gin bottle as his steward poured out the liberal measure that he had been taught to pour. 'Lots of chaps say that Plymouth isn't what it was, but I can't drink anything else. Pink?'

'Thank you, sir.'

'Well, Hallet, first of all I've to tell you that you've got a bar to that D.S.O. You've earned it. Shut up, you young ass. I hope to get a D.S.C. for your Number One and your Chief, and we may manage a mention for young Ferris. By the way: I've had a complaint about him, from some woman called Compton, in Kandy. But we'll talk about that another time. With any luck we'll get a decent allocation of medals for your Ship's Company: not a word, of course, until I've got it on paper.'

The S.O.O. began to murmur congratulations, but Meadows cut him short.

'Now, Hallet, where'll we send you this time? Somewhere nice and quiet, for a rest?'

'I don't think that 'd do any of us any good, sir. I'd like – may I make a suggestion, sir?'

'What the hell do you think I asked you for?'

'Well, sir, we can find our way through that minefield, now. There'd be some targets lower down.' Meadows grinned broadly, took a sip at his gin.

'What do you think, S.O.O.? Send him down to make a shemozzle off Malacca, eh?'

'I think it's a good idea, sir, so long as he comes out straight away when he's shown he's down there. Can't get caught hanging around in *that* alley.'

All right. Fix it. Steward! – fill these officers' glasses. And mine ... here's to you, Hallet.'

Half-past nine: Sub, in *Seahound*'s Wardroom, was busy with some official correspondence: there was more to be dealt with, and tonight, when he was Duty, was the time to get it done. But to hell, he thought, there are lots of duty nights to come. He shoved the papers back into their cardboard folders, slid the folders into a converted gas-mask locker. He had a new Peter Cheyney story that had arrived in the last post: he pulled it out of his drawer, settled himself in a corner and began to read about Slim Callaghan and the woman with long shapely legs and lots of money. This was undiluted escapism. They didn't fall like that, not in real life: you had to fight for them, one way or another.

He put the book down, wondered what the noise was about. That was Shadwell's voice: 'Why, y'little pimp, I'll kick y' flippin' — up y' flippin' —!' Feet rushing, shouts, Rogers shouting, 'Ar, shut it, Shaddy, for flip's sake!' A thud, more angry voices, a roar from Bird: 'Stow it, y' silly bastards!' A series of bangs that sounded like a man's head being thumped on the deck. The Sub leapt out of the wardroom, ran for'ard: where in hell was the Duty Petty Officer?

In the for'ard compartment, half-a-dozen men were fighting on the deck. Three of them were trying to hold down Shadwell: it took only one to hold the telegraphist, who was evidently the cause of the big torpedoman's displeasure.

'Get up, and stop that Goddamned row!'

The Sub was dwarfed when Shadwell, obeying the order, flung two men off his back and rose to his feet. The telegraphist, a man named Barney Rookes, stood panting heavily, his back to the bulkhead door. The Sub stood between them: he noticed a galley knife in the telegraphist's hand.

'Drop that knife, Rookes.'

'I wasn't going to use it, sir. I just 'ad it in me 'and.' Rookes' mouth was split and bleeding.

'Drop it.' The knife clattered on the iron deck under the torpedo racks. Shadwell growled,

'Like flip you wasn't goin' t' use it, yer dago bastard!'

'That's enough from you, Shadwell. Bird, where's the Duty P.O.?'

'Went inboard, sir. To fetch something.'

'Go and get him. Rookes, go and wait in the Control Room.'

'I didn't start it, sir.'

'I didn't say you did. Go aft.' The telegraphist lurched away. Chief Petty Officer Rawlinson dropped through the hatch. Sub moved out of the compartment, beckoned him. He walked aft as far as the Petty Officers' Mess.

'Where've you been?'

'Went up to the Mess, to get this book, sir.'

'You know damn well you've no business to leave the boat without my permission.'

'Yes, sir. I'm sorry, sir.'

'Shadwell and Rookes were fighting. Find out what it was all about, and report to me in the wardroom.'

'Aye aye, sir.'

The Sub sat down at the wardroom table, cursing quietly. Now both men would have to come up as defaulters: there was enough to do, enough to worry about, without this sort of thing.

Rawlinson reported. The telegraphist had knocked into Shadwell, who was writing a letter. Shadwell had cursed him, told him that just because he never wrote letters to his whore at home there was no call to go buggering up other people's letters. Rookes had assumed the term 'whore' to have been applied to his wife. He had grabbed the knife, which had been lying on the lockers, and had flung himself on Shadwell.

Shadwell said that he hadn't even known that Rookes had a wife. All he knew was that the bastard had a lot of pictures of naked women stuck up all over the Wireless Office: he didn't like Rookes, he said, and he reckoned that he'd bumped into him on purpose. Then Rookes had attacked him with a flippin' great knife, and he, Shadwell, had only defended himself.

'All right. Bring them up now. Rookes first.' He walked into the Control Room, heard Rawlinson bark,

'Telegraphist Rookes: get y' cap!'

One at a time they came before him: Rawlinson ordered, ''Shun! Off cap!' and read the charge.

'Anything to say?'

Each told his story, Rookes bitter, conscious of his battered face, Shadwell innocent and apparently shocked at the other man's rough behaviour.

'First Lieutenant's Report,' snapped the Sub. Tomorrow

morning they would see Number One, who would either deal with the matter himself or, if he thought the case more serious, pass it on to the Captain. Sub wondered if he couldn't save everyone a certain amount of trouble: he called the two men together, unofficially.

'Look,' he said. 'You'll both be seeing the First Lieutenant in the morning. Meantime, to save any more of this nonsense, listen to this.

'Rookes: Shadwell didn't know you were married. The word he used was not directed at anyone in particular. Do you accept that?'

Rookes muttered that he did. He had difficulty in moving his lips.

'Shadwell: Rookes thought you meant to insult his wife. If you'd thought that someone had used an expression like that about your wife, I reckon if you'd been the smaller man you'd have grabbed the nearest weapon and used it, eh?'

'No, sir. Well, I dunno, really.'

'Good God, man! Someone refers to your wife as a whore, and you don't do anything about it?'

Shadwell scratched the side of his head. 'Well, y' see, sir, in a manner o' speakin', she is.'

CHAPTER NINE

Once again, His Majesty's Submarine *Seahound* was about to sail from her base. Only one rope for'ard and one rope aft held her alongside, and as soon as the Captain came aboard and gave the order, these last links would be thrown off. Sub stood waiting on the for'ard casing: Bird, the Second Cox'n, stood massively beside him, coiling a heaving-line.

'Bit different to sailing from 'Oly Loch, ain't it, sir?'

It was, indeed. When they had left Scotland, just over a year ago, they had left foul weather, a gale and bursts of hail. A squall had lashed across the Loch just as they were slipping their ropes and wires, and some of the men, with the sailor's tendency towards superstition, had seen this as a bad omen for the future. But nothing had occurred to justify such fears, unless it had been the crossing of the Bay of Biscay in weather that made a misery of watch-keeping and a hell of everything except lying flat on your bunk, in that position with your knees up.

Bird muttered, 'Captain coming, sir.'

Sub moved aft to where the plank rested on the casing, waited there and saluted the Captain as he stepped on board and turned away to the bridge. Rogers murmured,

'All aboard the flippin' Skylark, trip rahnd the 'arbour 'alf a tanner!' Sub glared at him, shouted:

'Away plank!'

Two men of the Spare Crew, on the inside submarine, hauled it off. Number One yelled from the bridge, 'Let go aft!' and a minute later, as the stern swung out, 'Let go for'ard!' The ropes were thrown off the bollards, and the submarine backed away from the Depot Ship, driven by her electric motors. Clear of the side, she swung her bow away towards the harbour entrance, and at the same time her diesels roared into action. A shrill pipe was answered once more by the bugle on the high quarter-deck: gathering speed, *Seahound* headed for the open sea and the Malacca Straits.

'Well,' said the Captain, 'before we leave for the next patrol, Chief, we may have seen our wives. Number One: when do you plan to get married?'

'Not in a hurry, sir. When we get back to U.K. Think this war's going to last long, sir?'

'Don't ask me.' There had been a lot of rumours going around in Trincomali: one of an imminent Japanese surrender, and one of a Second Front being opened in Malaya. There was no doubt that the Fourteenth Army in Burma was moving steadily, rapidly forward: but there were always these rumours, in every ship, and they always started on the Mess-decks.

The Captain's cup and saucer began to slide slowly across the table. He pressed the bell for the messenger.

'Ask the Officer of the Watch what the weather's doing.'

'Aye aye, sir.' Presently the man returned.

'Officer of the Watch says it's blowing up a bit, sir.'

Number One patted the Engineer Officer on the shoulder.

'That's it, Chiefy: you're looking paler already.'

'You go to hell. Let's have the dice out, shall we?'

'Wants to take his mind off it,' observed Number One as he reached into the locker and brought out the dice.

'Ace up, King towards.' He flipped the dice with his finger: it trickled along a few inches and rested with the Ace on top again.

'Mine, by the looks of it.'

When the messenger of the Watch shook Sub at ten minutes to two in the morning and shouted in his ear that he was due to be on watch in ten minutes' time, Sub felt more than usually disinclined to leave his bunk. He was tired, and the violent motion of the submarine as she rose and fell to the sea left little doubt in his mind that this was one of the nights when a bunk was by far the best place. He tried to pretend that it was all a bad dream, this listening to the sea crashing on the hull over his head, but the messenger knew his job, and sharp at two o'clock Number One was delighted to hear the helmsman ask permission for the relief Officer of the Watch to come up. Number One, of course, was wide awake, and cheerful at the prospect of getting down to a cup of the Cox'n's cocoa before turning in for four lovely hours in his comfortable bunk, but his gay conversation was quite lost on the Sub, who had caught a bucketful of flying sea in his bleary face the moment he rose out of the hatch.

'Get your nose out, you old cow!' The bow digs deep into an enormous wave, then soars, flinging back a ton of salt water at the bridge. Sub ducks, cursing, cracks his head on the edge of the voice-pipe and curses more wildly as the water drenches him. Now the bow stands clear, the stern low and buried in the sea: a huge gulf opens ahead and the submarine swoops forward, her bow crashing down like a giant hammer. Bow up, roll to port: bow down, roll to starboard, swinging over until it looks as though she's going all the way. But she never does, she staggers for a moment then comes back fast while the bow swings up, up, high over the bridge while she stands on her tail and you hang on for your life. The sea crashes over, slams into the bridge and bursts like flying shrapnel up through the holes in the platform.

It's strange to think that at other times you feel like a trespasser, spoiling the smooth flat mirror of the ocean. This is the sea as you know her when her mood is bad, and you know all the moods she has. She's like the girl in that song that the sailors sing, a fascinating bitch. A bitch that has the devil's temper, and she lets it rip whenever she feels like it. Look down at the bow, at that crazy hammer-head that swings in a great arc up and down a dozen times a minute. Inside that thing are men asleep in their hammocks: asleep, in that! At home they used to pay sixpence a time to have that done to them in a fun-fair: at home they were woken if the wind flapped a curtain in the bedroom.

Keep your watch. This is your life, the one you chose.

The sea had changed her mood when the submarine approached the entrance to the Straits, two days later. Not a ripple, not a single streak of white showed that twenty-four hours earlier this placid beauty had been a chaos of pounding waves and flying foam. She was the Indian Ocean again: she had worn herself out pretending to be the North Atlantic.

'Why don't you get a new pipe, Chief?' The Captain looked critically at his Engineer Officer's briar, which had half the mouthpiece bitten off.

'I like this one,' answered Chief, with his usual simplicity.

'What made you bite the end off? Lose your temper?'

'Well, it's rather a long story, really. And I don't think I ought to tell it, with this youngster here ... sorry, Sub, I was forgetting you'd come of age.'

'Let's have it, Chiefy.' Chief thumbed down the mixture of Admiralty Issue and Three Nuns, and said,

'I was training at Keyham at the time.' He struck a match, and puffed hard at the blackened object in his mouth. 'Very young and inexperienced. I'd been rather flirting with a bit of stuff called Elsie, who used to dish out fish and chips in a café that we used quite often. Nice-looking girl. Well, we decided, three or four of us, including old Batchy Wilson, who went down in the Med., to have a party. Took the girls out to dinner and dance in some local dive. Mind you, I'd had practically nothing to do with women. Nothing much, anyway. Party ended: I was quite sober. She asked me to see her home to her flat, so I did, and she asked me to come in for a cup of coffee. Nothing else entered my head, you know: it was bloody cold, and coffee sounded just the job.

'We went up, and she said she was just going into the kitchen to put the coffee on. I sat down and lit my pipe: this one. A few minutes later I heard her coming into the room, and I looked up, expecting to hear her say that the coffee wouldn't be long, or something of that sort. But she didn't say a word. Just stood there. And she'd taken all her clothes off.'

Chief puffed strongly at the jagged mouthpiece.

'That,' he said, 'was when I bit through the stem of this ancient burner.'

They were silent for a moment. Then Number One said,

'I suppose you thanked her for a lovely evening and shook her warmly by the hand on the way out.'

'As a matter of fact, I did, more or less. I felt sort of shell-shocked, you know.'

The Captain was looking steadily at Chief.

'Chief,' he said, slowly, 'you're either a born liar, or a bloody fool.'

Southwards again through the Malacca Straits, slowly and very quietly southwards into the bottleneck. By now it's all routine, not only the patrol and the watch-keeping but also the boarding, the Gun Action: all of it is taken as a matter of course, performed easily, effortlessly, with quiet efficiency.

The dentist's drill in the middle of the night, the harsh buzzing of the Night Alarm. It's hardly necessary to wake up: you could do it in your sleep. Gear ready, wait. The order, 'Boarding Party on the Bridge.' Up the ladder, the thin rungs biting into the rubber soles of your shoes which were designed to be worn on a tennis-court. Tennis: they'll be playing, now, in Sussex, in the soft English summer while they wait for the war to end. For most of them it's ended already, ended on the day they called 'VE Day', and that night the people danced in the streets of London, Lewes, Hastings: the little pub at Pevensey was full, so you'd heard. You'd heard too that they gave a cocktail party at home that night, no doubt on the war-time civilian lines where the only drink was a cocktail that was less alcoholic even than war-time beer. Some beer was not so bad, though, when you could get an occasional pint of 'Old' which the landlord kept for his friends and regular patrons. Remember Mr Oast, who kept the Ram's Horn and was always glad to see you when you were home on leave? Dear old Mr Oast, so proud of his son in the Hartillery, in Foreign Parts.

'VE Night': that was the night you sank two junks, and one of the Chinese came up to you afterwards in the Control Room, bowed and smiled, handed you a grubby card with his name printed on it: 'High Class Officers' and Gentlemen's Outfitting' it said underneath, and gave an address in Singapore. He had wanted to come back to Trinco with you, and he had been very upset when you put him in a fishing-boat instead. That was 'VE Night'.

You're on the bridge with your belt round your waist, the ·38 and the bayonet heavy at your side. You peer for'ard between the Captain and the Navigator, who was on watch when he sighted the junk, and you study the dim shape ahead. It looks big, and you think it may have a Jap guard on board: the big ones very often have, although nowadays they're getting short of Japs and it's always a surprise to meet one. No pleasure in the meeting.

'Down you go,' comes the Captain's order, and you slide down the side and take your men up for'ard, warning them again to crouch down so that the Captain can see over their heads and so that you present a smaller target in case it's a booby-trap with a machine-gun. That has been known, and also the trap of a guard with a bunch of grenades which he tries to lob into the hatch as the submarine draws alongside.

'Slower, for Christ's sake!' you think to yourself as the junk looms closer too fast, but the Captain can't see very well in the moonless night, and there's a hell of a crash as you touch. Before the crash you jumped, and now you're there on the junk, thuds behind you as the Boarding Party follow. You jump to the door of the cabin, but the Chinese crew are in the way, yelling blue murder and getting knocked over in the rush. You've missed the Jap guard, who has come round the other side of the shelter and moves towards Shadwell, tugging at the automatic on his belt. Shadwell is quicker than the Jap and shoots him dead before the gun is more than half-way up. You rush out to do something useful when you hear the shots, but you see at once that there's nothing to be done. Shadwell says, 'It's all right, sir,' and you go back to collect the papers. If Shadwell says it's all right, it is all right.

Only routine from then on, only drill as you place the charge, but there's a slip in the drill when you find that there's nothing movable to put on top of the charge before you leave it. It's necessary to tamp it down, to make sure that the blast of the explosion goes downwards through the bottom of the junk and not upwards where it's wasted. Shadwell is with you, tries to shift one of the big crates, but it's too heavy.

''Alf a mo, sir,' he mutters, and climbs quickly up out of the hold, drops back again with the body of the dead Jap.

'This'll do, sir.'

'Clear the junk!' you yell, and they go, Bird just ahead of Shadwell. You jump back into the dark hold, set fire to the fuse and lug the body over on top of the charge. Shadwell had picked up that corpse like a baby, but you find it as much as you can lift.

Back on deck, you jump for the casing, flash the torch as a signal to the Captain and hurry aft in the dark as the submarine backs away from the junk which hasn't long to float.

As usual it seems a long time before the bang, and before it comes the Captain looks irritably round at you as though you've bungled the job. But you haven't, not this time or any other. The junk lifts with the blast and drops back smack in the water as you lean quickly over the side of the bridge and bring up your supper. It was a picture in your mind that did that, a picture of the Jap with his stomach blown out of his back: you know what guts look like, because you saw what happened to Wilkins, and so you've been sick down the side of the bridge, on to the swelling curve of the saddle-tanks. The mess won't matter: when the submarine dives before dawn, it'll be washed off in the same way that Wilkins' blood was. The sea is clever at cleaning things up. What matters is that you needed to be sick: after all, you've come of age, you're twenty-one.

In the for'ard Mess, at breakfast next morning, Rogers looked reprovingly at Shadwell.

'Shaddy,' he said, shaking his head, 'I 'as to mention that wot 'as come to my ears about your flippin' bloodthirsty carry-on last night causes me no end of displeasure.'

'Ar, eat y' flippin' bangers, an' shut up. Flippin' windbag, that's all you are.'

'Last night, Shaddy, you done a thing as you may well regret. 'Ow'd you like to think in a few months as 'ow you'd shot a poor little co-belligerent, eh?'

'Co-belligerer be flipped. It was a flippin' Jap, and 'e'd 'a conked me if I 'adn't 'a swiped 'im first.'

'Remember when we was in the Med. together, Shaddy, the go we 'ad with them Eye-Ties off Spartivento? When they near finished us?'

'What of it?'

'Six months after that they was dear little co-belligerents, see?

Now these Japs: you'll 'ave 'eard the buzz as they're goin' t' jag in soon?'

'I 'eard a buzz, but I dunno where it come from.'

'Never mind where it flippin' well come from, Shaddy. You mark my words: come six months, they'll be flippin' co-belligerents.'

Shadwell looked contemptuously at his shipmate.

'Don't be soft. There ain't nobody left to belligerate against.'

''Ow about the Ruskies?'

'Wot, Uncle Joe? You're daft. You're flippin' well barmy, d'ye hear?'

Early morning: the Sub lay on his bunk, knowing that in half-an-hour he would be called to take over the watch. The submarine was south of the minefields, nosing in at periscope depth towards the port of Malacca. From the remarks and orders that he could hear from the Control Room, where the Navigator had the watch and the Captain was keeping an eye on the approach, Sub gathered that the morning fog was still thick: he could picture the woolly blanket encircling the upper lens of the periscope, the water shining as though it had been wiped with an oily rag. He heard the Captain's breathing as he leant over the chart-table, heard him softly curse the low visibility.

There ought to be something worth sinking, down here. No submarine had been here for a long time: it was as though they had been given the first licence to shoot in what had been a game preserve. The Captain was keyed up, anticipating a target: Sub thought, I ought to be, too. He felt as Chief always professed to feel: what in hell did it matter if there was a target or if there was nothing? It was the low mood, one of the times when you looked round and noticed how squalid the surroundings really were: you thought of other men fighting in the open air, living more normally, not creeping about, eating and sleeping and peering through a blasted tube at the empty sea. The jokes were stale, the news was old, breakfast was always the same, hurried at that when it had to be gulped down quickly in order to take over a dreary watch.

164

Dreary? This was virgin territory, from a submariner's point of view: it should be anything but dreary. Well, all right, perhaps there'd be something to sink. When it had been sunk they'd go back through the minefield, hang around looking for junks until the recall came. Two hours on and four hours off: sausages for breakfast, corned beef for lunch, sardines for tea and some revolting thing for supper. He rolled over, knowing that when he'd been on watch for half-an-hour this depression would be gone: so would the fog, lifting to reveal the entrance to the port. Perhaps also to reveal a target.

He thought, I might as well turn out now, clean my teeth: there was a horrible taste in his mouth. Probably, he thought, I have halitosis: must be rather unpleasant for everyone else. He swung his legs off the bunk, groped for his shoes under the wardroom table. He was trying to force his left foot into the right shoe, when he heard Saunders report Hydrophone Effect. He heard the Captain drop the dividers on the chart table, heard his voice saying for the millionth time, urgently:

'Up periscope.'

Silence now, while he tied the laces on his shoes, tightened the belt of his shorts. He stood up, shook Jimmy's elbows: the First Lieutenant opened his eyes, stared unrecognizingly at him.

'Something happening, Number One. Probably Diving Stations in a minute.' Number One began to climb off his bunk, muttering.

They heard the Captain's voice again:

'Can't see anything. Are you sure it's H.E.?'

'Yes, sir.' Saunders' voice. 'Green three-oh, sir, moving left to right.'

The Captain grunted, continued his search. Number One said:

'If this turns out to be bugger-all, Sub, I'll fix you. I'll —'

'Diving Stations! Stand by Gun Action!' Sub felt the old shiver in his stomach as he flung himself out of the wardroom.

'Down periscope.' The Captain grinned, rubbed the side of his jaw. 'It's that Tank Landing Ship again, Sub.'

The one they had missed last time they met it. The one with a big gun on the stern. The one that had an air escort, last time.

'Up periscope. Range ... that! I'm on his starboard quarter.

Enemy speed nine. Group up, starboard ten.'

Sub worked the handles on the calculating machine, lining up the dials. He got the deflection, passed it to the Sightsetter. The Gun's Crew were ready, sleep still in their eyes, but that made no odds because they'd done this before in their sleep.

Sub remembered the first Gun Action of them all, the one against the trawler off Port Blair: he had felt scared stiff, himself, and seeing the apprehensive looks on the faces of the Gun's Crew he had told them not to worry: only a trawler, he had said, this'd be easy. They'd never done it before, except on a practice shoot, and on a practice shoot there were never any shore batteries to shoot back. 'Gun's Crew closed up, sir.'

'Very good. Group down. Up periscope.'

They waited tensely while the Captain took a final check. He jerked up the handles of the periscope, stepped back, and the long, brass tube hissed down into its well.

'Fifty feet. Group up, full ahead together.' The deck angled under their feet and the hum of the motors rose under the full power of the batteries.

'Fifty feet, sir.'

'Stand by to surface.' Orders, reports.

'Ready to surface, sir.'

'Surface!' Sub sprang on to the ladder behind the Captain, heard the air smack into the tanks. Number One stood under the hatch, his hands on the side of the ladder. He shouted,

'Forty feet! ... Thirty! ... twenty-five! ... twenty!' and then his whistle shrieked: Sub, craning his neck to look up, saw the Captain fling the hatch back. Behind the Captain, Sub scrambled up into the light, the dripping bridge. He took his weight on his hands on the cab at the front of the bridge, jumped up, swung his legs over: below him, the gun was swinging round towards the enemy, the breech was open and a shell was coming out of the hatch in the hands of the leading member of the Ammunition Supply Party. The Loader grabbed it, slammed it into the breech, the sights were on and the Gunlayer pressed his trigger. Watch for the fall of shot: Sub strained his eyes at the sea around the enemy.

Splash, left. 'Right eight, shoot!' Another round crashed away, and a flash from the enemy's stern was the sign of her first shot in reply. At least this was better than the last time, from the point of view of weather conditions: *Seahound*'s second shot fell short, in line.

'Up eight hundred, shoot!' Sub ignored the sound of the enemy shell passing overhead.

'Down four hundred, shoot!' That last shot of the enemy's had fallen in their wake: the Captain bent to the voice-pipe, shouted for an increase in speed and put the wheel over to starboard. The Trainer slowly turned his wheel, keeping the gun trained on the enemy as the submarine altered course.

'That's the stuff, Sub!' Yes, a hit, a lovely sight, only it'll take a lot more than just one hit to finish the business: the Tank Landing Ship is all of thirteen hundred tons.

'No correction, shoot!' Another shell from the enemy fell on the submarine's starboard quarter: *Seahound* was firing three shells for every two of the enemy's.

A cheer from the bridge: a third hit. The Captain believed in giving encouragement when it was deserved: if that one had missed, thought the Sub, he'd have wondered what the hell I was doing.

'No correction, shoot!' The empty, scorched cylinder clanged out of the breech on to the gun-deck: already the breech was closed behind another shell.

That was the right sort of hit! A hit on the enemy's gun: that gun had fired its last shell.

'Point of aim, the water-line!' The Sub could never hear his own voice after a few rounds had been fired, and he was constantly surprised to find that his orders were heard and obeyed at the gun. Up here, on the front edge of the bridge, the blast from each shell fired had a blinding, deafening effect.

The Gunlayer fired a moment sooner than he had intended: the sights were half-way up the enemy stern instead of on the waterline. The shell crashed in through the high stern, right the way through, exploded in a stern compartment which the Japs had recently converted to hold a cargo of mines. There were a dozen mines in the compartment, and as one they exploded with the shell, not an explosion, an eruption: the enemy ship was split open, her bowels flung into the sky. *Seahound*'s Gun's Crew stood back from their gun shielding their eyes and staring in stunned amazement at the havoc of flying debris, the huge billowing cloud of smoke and the shooting tongue of orange flame.

'Cor stone the crows!' muttered the Gunlayer. 'Did we do that?'

As the Gun's Crew secured the gun and cleared the gun-deck of shell-cases, *Seahound* swung round and headed northwards up the Straits. The sky was still full of dirt: Sub looked up at the lighthouse on the tall headland, and thought that they'd given someone a good morning's entertainment. It must have been quite a spectacle, from up there. He saw the hatch shut over the Gunlayer's head, and at the same time he thought he heard the Captain shout into the voice-pipe,

'Stand by Boarding Party!'

There wasn't anything left of the Tank Landing Ship. He must have heard wrong: his ears were still ringing from the noise of the battle.

The Captain spoke to him. 'Go down and get your gear, Sub.' He pointed at a big junk, creeping into sight round the headland.

The Sub thought, as he obeyed the order, that the Captain was showing signs of over-confidence: a boarding in daylight, in these waters! But when the time came, it was dead easy, no opposition, no Jap guard, and the sky stayed empty. The Chinese crew even helped Sub and his men to climb on board, welcome guests. The cargo was rice, sugar and matches; Sub sent a crate of matches across to the submarine.

He had fired the charge and was about to abandon the junk when he heard the Captain shouting something, pointing at the bow of the junk. Sub hurried for'ard, looking around: a small, ginger kitten ran towards him, mewing. He scooped it up, ran aft and swung himself down to the submarine.

A minute later, *Seahound* was speeding away into the deep water: then the vents dropped open, the spray plumed up and she dived to periscope depth. Someone was likely to resent the intrusion and the damage, and if she stayed in these waters there would very likely be some trouble: the Captain turned her north, up towards the gap in the minefields. This would be the fourth time that she had passed through them: when you've done it once, it's easy.

Every ship and submarine on the Station had a secret chart, now, with a track marked on it, the track through the minefield that *Seahound* found.

Sometimes, when you lay on your bunk and there was nothing very much to think about, it was pleasant to think about going home. Perhaps it wouldn't be long, now: it was not, thought the Captain, that he felt any great urge to be back in England, it was the actual journey home that he looked forward to. A sort of holiday cruise, visits to places on the way: Aden, Port Said, perhaps Alexandria: Malta and Gibraltar. Yes, it'd be a lot of fun.

Strange, he thought, that he should like a place like Aden: hot and sandy, nothing much to do except swim and drink, yet the place had a certain atmosphere that made a short visit attractive. Port Said: a dance at the Eastern Exchange, just for the hell of it. Alexandria: the Auberge Bleu, slumming at the Monseigneur. He wondered if Louise still lived in Alexandria and if she still had the fat and aged Egyptian for a husband.

Malta: the centre of many submariners' memories. It was in Malta that he had struck that policeman, it was the Malta flotilla that had sunk over a million tons of Rommel's supplies: the memories swam together, the wild days ashore and the wilder weeks at sea.

Gibraltar: the flat on Scud Hill. The night they rolled up the carpet and launched it out of the window so that it fell on a policeman who was standing in the road protesting against the noise. Another carpet had been their ticket to a free evening in the best hotel: the Captain had been a Sub, then. He and two others had taken the carpet and carried it out of the hotel foyer. Then they telephoned the Manager, told him that they had recognized his new red carpet, the pride of his heart, that they had taken it by force from two men who had it on a cart and were trying to sell it. The Manager had been most grateful, had given them a dinner on the house, and after the dinner and cigars they had walked out of the hotel carrying a champagne bucket.

The Captain wondered whether that champagne bucket was still among the other trophies in the flat on Scud Hill. He couldn't do that sort of thing nowadays of course, not even if he wanted to: but it would be good to see the old places again, recognize the barmen's faces, a final night or two with Louise before he settled down to marriage and life-long fidelity.

The Captain fell asleep, while *Seahound*'s motors drove her gently up the Straits, towards the mines.

Two days later, the Depot Ship in Trincomali was in a state of wild excitement. It was one little point in a vast area of elation, victory. The Japanese High Command had signalled its unconditional surrender. The yellow horde that had blazed a path of murder and brutality across the East, at first almost unopposed, had been beaten to its knees. An atom bomb had given them the excuse to admit defeat, to save something from the wreckage by kneeling to an adversary whose own ideas of human and military conduct they had scorned when the power was in their animal hands.

In the Staff Office, during the afternoon, the Staff Officer, Operations, drafted signals ordering all submarines on patrol to return forthwith, reporting their positions and estimated times-of-arrival at Trincomali. *Seahound* was the only submarine in the Malacca Straits, and in the signal to her was included the information that on her way back up the Straits she would meet surface forces which were at that moment on their way into the Straits, on their way to accept the surrender of Singapore.

The submarines would be dived all day, knowing nothing of the surrender which had come so suddenly, and the signals would reach them that night, when they surfaced for the night patrol.

The Staff Officer, Operations, leant back in his chair and shut his eyes. In his mind he heard a speech, a speech that told of defeat. He had been a passenger in a troopship rounding the Cape, bound for Suez: it was early in 1942. One evening they were all assembled in the dark, blacked-out recreation space, to hear a special broadcast from London. In grave, simple words the Prime Minister told them of the fall of Singapore. The Staff Officer, Operations, remembered the shock that the news had given them, but he remembered also the hard determination to win in spite of this and any other loss, a determination with which the strength and personal courage of the speaker had inspired them.

Now, the ships were going back. It had taken a long time, but they were going back.

'Have you passed the last signals yet?'

It was half-past nine in the evening, and he was speaking over the telephone from the Staff Office.

'All but one, sir. We haven't got hold of *Seahound* yet.'

'Keep on trying until you do. Then ring through to me here.'

'Aye aye, sir,'

He leant forward over the desk, his head on his hands. Staff Officers are hard-worked people at times like this. Odd, *Seahound* not answering: she should have surfaced, by now. Still, there were many possible reasons for the delay. He fell asleep at his desk, his forehead resting on his clasped hands. He was more tired than he knew: in that position he slept soundly, undisturbed for over an hour, while below in the wardroom and on the messdecks a thousand men sang songs and face with a fantastic faith the Peace that lay ahead.

Suddenly a noise outside, the crack of a rocket exploding over the harbour as someone started a private celebration of the victory, woke him. He looked at his watch: eleven o'clock! Perhaps he had failed to hear the telephone, perhaps they had forgotten his orders. He picked up the receiver and rang through to the Communications Office.

'That signal got through to *Seahound*?'

'No, sir.'

'Keep on trying. All night, if necessary.'

'Aye aye, sir.'

Frowning, assuming that expression of annoyance to hide the fear inside him, the Staff Officer, Operations, hurried down to report to Captain Meadows.

In the Wireless Office, a telegraphist sat at his bench, tapping out *Seahound*'s call-sign again and again. From time to time another man took over, gravely, realizing the import, tapping out the dots and dashes, visualizing the little wireless cabinet in the submarine, seeing clearly the face of his friend at the other side of the ocean. Behind the operators, a Chief Petty Officer Telegraphist paced up and down, a cigarette stuck on his lower lip and a frown on his lined face. He was thinking all the time,

'Should 'a got her, by now.'

After midnight, the Commanding Officer of His Majesty's Submarine *Slayer* stepped over the gangway on to the Depot Ship's quarter-deck. He and some others had decided to do their celebrating ashore, had caught a boat and called on the Wren Officers' Mess with some bottles concealed in rolled bathing-towels. It had been a quiet evening: they sat on the veranda with the Wrens, and talked, remembered old times and tried to believe that it was all really over. For so many years they had thought about this day, and now it had come so suddenly that it seemed unreal.

He went up the ladder from the quarter-deck, and as he reached the top he saw the figure of the S.O.O., who was standing at the ship's side staring out over the water in the direction of the harbour entrance. *Slayer*'s Captain tapped him on the shoulder.

'Wotcher, Stinky!' The other man turned quickly, and seeing his face the young submarine Captain caught his breath and hesitated a moment before he asked, quietly,

'What's wrong?'

'*Seahound*. All the recall signals are through except hers. She can't have surfaced.'

'Oh, Christ.' What could you say, to a thing like that? They turned and walked together along the deck, down on to the welldeck and up to the Staff Office. The S.O.O. picked up the receiver.

'Anything?'

'No, sir. Nothing.'

'Keep trying.' He turned to the younger man. 'Why don't you go and turn in? You can't do anything. You look pretty tired.'

'Me, tired? You look half dead. And what can you do? ... Have you got any cigarettes?'

*

Number One had never seen such rain in his life. It was practically solid water: it could have been coming up out of the sea, as easily as falling out of the clouds: there was so much rain that it was difficult to see where it started and where it ended. It fell steadily, furiously, pounding and drumming on the casing and in the bridge, deadening the rumble of the diesels. Deadening sight, as well as sound: visibility was only about forty yards. Number One leaned against the front of the bridge, straining his eyes into the night. If anything was sighted, it'd be sighted at a range of forty yards, and that wouldn't leave much time for thinking things out....

The Captain stood beside him. His presence annoyed Number One. On watch, he liked to be alone, like the film-star. Because the visibility was low, the Captain had come up and stayed up, as though he doubted his First Lieutenant's ability to deal with any sudden emergency. But it was only a superficial annoyance to Jimmy: he knew that if he were in command, he'd be doing the same thing.

The Captain lowered his dripping face to the rim of the voice pipe.

'Control Room!'

'Control Room.'

'Ask the P.O.Tel. how long he's going to be with that blasted set.'

'Aye aye, sir.' The Cox'n, who was on watch, lumbered aft the short distance to the wireless office.

'Ain't you found that flippin' fault yet, Sparks? Captain wants to know 'ow long.'

The P.O. Telegraphist had his head inside a grey metal cabinet. He was fiddling at something there with a screwdriver.

'Ger,' he answered. 'Flip orf.'

'Can't tell the Captain that, Sparky. 'Ow long?'

The P.O.Tel's long body began creeping slowly, feet first, out from under the bench. When he got his head out, he sat up and glared at the Cox'n.

'Tell 'im the flipper's fixed.' As the Cox'n vanished into the Control Room, the telegraphist heaved himself to his feet and began tuning his receiver. He slid headphones over his ears, and settled down on the seat. It was hot and stuffy in the cabinet: it smelt of switches and fuses and valves. Several half-naked women smirked down at him from their positions on the thin, steel partition. He reached for a stub of pencil, and began to write down the jumble of code.

Presently he pressed the buzzer, and the Control Room messenger stuck his head round the door.

'Eh?'

'Tell the Captain – urgent signal addressed to us. Cipher.' The messenger met the Captain as he stepped off the ladder, soaked to the skin.

'All right. Give it to the Engineer Officer.' He heard Chief's angry mutterings as the messenger woke him and gave him the signal.

'Urgent, sir.'

'Urgent be damned.' But all the same, he sat up and reached for his code-books.

A minute later, the Captain arrived in the wardroom. He leant one wet hand flat on the table, and eased himself sideways on to the locker.

'Well, Chief?' The Engineer seemed to be having some difficulty. Wide-eyed and open-mouthed, he was goggling at the sheet of paper in his hand. He looked up at the Captain.

'It's – it's —' He couldn't say it. The Captain grabbed the signal from him. A look of complete astonishment crossed his face. Then, quickly, he remembered that it would be better to give the impression of having expected something of the sort. After six years...!

'Well, Chief. No more bangs, eh?' Chief still hadn't found control of his tongue. He shook the Sub's shoulder, and when he woke, mouthed at him excitedly.

'What in hell's the matter with you?'

'He's trying to tell you that the war's over. Japs have jagged in, Sub.' The young man stared, trying to get it into his head.

'Oh ... I see.' He paused, looking at the Captain. He didn't know whether he was glad of this or not. He supposed that it would be expected of everybody to be pleased. He remembered that he was still tired and that soon he'd be called for his watch, war or no war. He lay down again, and closed his eyes.

'Thought your pains had started, or something, Chief,' he

murmured, and chuckled to himself, already half-way back to sleep. The Captain wrote out a short signal, and handed it to Chief.

'Fix it up and send it off.'

On the bridge it was still raining hard. The Captain heaved himself out of the hatch, and stood beside his First Lieutenant.

'Come round to three-one-five, Number One. Four hundred revs.' Number One raised one hand in acknowledgement, and passed the order down the voice-pipe. The Captain shouted in his ear,

'Just got a signal. Japs have hurled in. We're going home!'

Jimmy peered at him through the driving rain.

'I don't believe it!'

'All right, don't. And don't relax the look-out. It takes two to declare peace.' The Captain dropped through the hatch and down the ladder into the Control Room. He shook off the loose water, and reached for the microphone of the broadcasting system. Flicking the switch on, he tested by slapping the face of the instrument and hearing the thumping echo in the loudspeakers.

'D'ye hear, there? ... D'ye hear, there?' The men on watch stood in a close group, the dim light glowing on their unshaven faces. The helmsman craned his neck round to stare at the Captain.

'D'ye hear, there? This is the Captain speaking. Shake your messmates and get round the loudspeakers....'

Up for'ard, Shadwell grinned to himself. He enjoyed shaking Rogers. He leaned over the hammock, grabbed his friend's right eat, twisting and pulling at the same time. Rogers woke with his fists swinging out of the hammock: a stream of oaths ripped across the compartment.

'Now, now!' murmured Shadwell, soothingly. ''Ush, ducky. We want to 'ear what the Captain 'as to say, not what you've bin dreaming about.' The Captain's voice came at them again from the speaker.

'I've an important announcement to make...'

The moon broke through a rift in the rain-clouds, gleamed on

Seahound's shiny black hull. She crashed her bow into the gentle waves, flinging them aside one after the other, tossing them in gleaming showers of spray over her steel shoulders. Number One paused for a moment in his looking-out, and watched the regular fist-slamming impact of the powerful bow as it broke steadily through, and while he watched that easy effortless motion he thought to himself that this was the way it had always been, with *Seahound*. She took it all so quietly. The North Atlantic at its worst had flung its weight against her: a Burma hurricane had raved and torn at her in its crazy rage. Germans had bombed her, and Japanese had shelled her: she had known the roar and the clanging blows of Italian depth-charges. The only thing she hadn't known was Peace: and that, thought Number One, shocking himself with the truth, would be the end of the road, the scrap-heap. They'd swarm all over her, cutting with flame and steel, hacking and tearing her apart because she had served her purpose and was of no further use. Feeling the lift of her under his feet and watching the way she slammed into the waves, he thought: You'll take this in your stride, too, you lovely, courageous old bitch! Smoothing along to the breakers' yard, with your head in the air! Ruthless and vicious, uncomfortable to live in, stinking of shale oil and sometimes of things much worse, I'd give everything I have to save you. His hand rested on the curved timber that edged the top of the bridge, and the tip of his thumb felt the nick that had been made a year ago when they were loading spare engine parts and the crane-driver carelessly swung a heavy part against the bridge. He knew every inch of his ship.

He looked down at her bow again, and he thought: You don't give a damn, do you? You won't mind being scrapped. They'll tear you up and make your steel into cars and tractors and cutlery, and maybe one day I'll ride a bicycle and it'll be a part of you.

Whatever they make of you, he thought, it'll be good.